BEING BILLY

phil earle

PENGUIN BOOKS

PENGUIN BOOKS

Published by the Penguin Group
Penguin Books Ltd, 80 Strand, London WC2R ORL, England
Penguin Group (USA) Inc., 375 Hudson Street, New York, New York 10014, USA
Penguin Group (Canada), 90 Eglinton Avenue East, Suite 700, Toronto, Ontario, Canada M4P 2Y3
(a division of Pearson Penguin Canada Inc.)
Penguin Ireland, 25 St Stephen's Green, Dublin 2, Ireland (a division of Penguin Books Ltd)
Penguin Group (Australia), 250 Camberwell Road, Camberwell, Victoria 3124, Australia
(a division of Pearson Australia Group Pty Ltd)
Penguin Books India Pvt Ltd, 11 Community Centre, Panchsheel Park, New Delhi – 110 017, India
Penguin Group (NZ), 67 Apollo Drive, Rosedale, North Shore 0632, New Zealand
(a division of Pearson New Zealand Ltd)
Penguin Books (South Africa) (Pty) Ltd, 24 Sturdee Avenue, Rosebank, Johannesburg 2196, South Africa

Penguin Books Ltd, Registered Offices: 80 Strand, London WC2R ORL, England

penguin.com

First published 2011
006

Text copyright © Phil Earle, 2011
'Please, Please, Please, Let Me Get What I Want', words and music by Steven Morrissey and Johnny
Marr, copyright © Artemis Muziekuitgeverij B.V. (BUM/STE). All rights on behalf of Artemis
Muziekuitgeverij B.V. administered by Warner/Chappell Artemis Music Ltd.
All rights reserved

Set in 10.5/15.5pt Sabon
Typeset by Palimpsest Book Production Limited, Falkirk, Stirlingshire
Made and printed in Great Britain by Clays Ltd, St Ives plc

British Library Cataloguing in Publication Data
A CIP catalogue record for this book is available from the British Library

ISBN: 978-0-141-33135-5

www.greenpenguin.co.uk

Para Laura (¿para quién si no?), por 1999, por los tiempos locos que lo precedieron y por la felicidad que siguió después ...

This book is also dedicated to the Sailors children, wherever you are ...

Haven't had a dream in a long time
See, the life I've had
Can make a good man bad

So for once in my life
Let me get what I want
Lord knows, it would be the first time
Lord knows, it would be the first time

'Please, Please, Please, Let Me Get What I Want' –
The Smiths

PROLOGUE

The light in the hall gave the game away.

Eleven p.m. and it was still on. If they were home, they would be in bed and all the lights would be off.

No, I knew this meant they were away. Even if they had gone to the pub, they'd have been back. Work tomorrow and all that.

I scuttled towards the front door, trying to stick to the shadows, turning the rock over in my hand. But as I reached the door, I decided to try the key. Don't know why. After all, it'd been years since I left. Surely they'd have changed the locks? They weren't the sort to take risks. They'd made that only too clear.

So when the key turned in the lock I was pretty stunned.

Not wanting to draw attention to the open door, I chucked the rock back on to the garden and stepped inside, closing the door quietly.

Leaning against the wall, I shut my eyes and listened.

Aside from the ticking clock and the humming of the fridge – silence.

It was beyond perfection. Slipping off my trainers, I

picked my way along the hall, smiling as I clocked the timer switch on the lamp.

I popped my head around the door of the kitchen and dining room. Nothing had changed. It was as if time had stopped three years ago and had only kicked in when I'd closed the front door seconds ago.

I reached the lounge, but paused when my hand touched the door handle. Something stopped me from going in. Memories, I suppose. Too much had gone on in that room and none of it good.

Instead, I turned to the stairs and crawled up them, keeping my head below the level of the window on the landing. You never knew who was twitching their curtains, even late at night.

I didn't pause at the top of the stairs.

I knew where I wanted to go.

Why I was here.

I padded past the photos of Jan and Grant that still hung on the wall, past the cheap tasteless prints that they loved, to the bedroom door.

Without pausing, I pushed my way inside, and suddenly my senses were on fire.

Even though everything about the room was different, it still felt the same. It still felt like mine.

The posters had gone of course, only tiny traces of Blu-Tack remained, pockmarking the wall at irregular intervals. Grant never did finish jobs properly.

Everything was neutral. The bedding, curtains, even the carpet, a deathly beige. It was as if the only way they could reclaim the room from me was to make everything completely nondescript. A blank canvas.

It didn't matter. I knew where I was. When I closed my eyes, I could still see the City team photo stuck above my bed. Still hear the music pumping out from the windowsill. Still smell the overpowering whiff of Lynx deodorant.

I allowed myself a smile as I fell on to the bed, and as my head sank into the pillow I felt the first of the knots untie in my stomach.

Slowly, slowly, slowly, knot after knot after knot released. I could feel the tension lifting out of me, like it was fog rising. And with it came clarity, and for the first time in months, maybe years, I allowed sleep to come without fighting it.

Because I knew where I was.

I knew I was safe.

I knew I was home.

CHAPTER 1

I should have realized they'd call the police when they found me missing.

Unfortunately, this didn't dawn on me until I was face down on the hallway floor, arms pinned at my sides, crucifixion-style.

'You're really getting a buzz out of this, aren't you?' I spat at them. 'This what you do when you're not on duty, pin down kids for kicks?'

'If you think we're enjoying this, Billy, then you are sadly mistaken,' rasped the Colonel, the strain showing in his voice. 'As soon as you calm down, then we'll be happy to let go. But while you're angry, we have no option but to hold you. It's for your own good.'

I knew the drill, had been here more times in the last eight years than I cared to remember, but I wasn't ready to calm down. I wanted to hurt them in some way.

Any way I could.

So I let my breathing slow, muscles relaxing in the process. At first their grip remained tight, forcing my wrists and ankles into the floor, but after about thirty seconds, I felt the pressure on my left arm relax.

It wasn't the Colonel. He knew me too well. He was hanging on for round two.

It was the other guy, the new bod, all social-work speak and sympathetic smiles.

He made the mistake of getting into range, craning round into my eyeline, trying to talk me all the way down.

Big mistake.

Instinctively, I let one go at him. Not a lungful. Not my greatest effort. But enough to catch him flush in the face as he began to speak.

Caught *him* off guard in a big way, but not the Colonel.

As the newbie stumbled away in disgust, my arm went instantly up my back, forcing my head straight back into the floor.

'That's ENOUGH, Billy!' he yelled into my ear.

'Then tell the scum to keep away from me. I don't need to hear his university bollocks.'

I felt my arm go further up my back.

'They teach you this move in the army, Ronnie?' I gasped. 'Good to know you were a decent soldier, cos you're a crappy carer.'

'Blimey, thanks, Bill.' Although I couldn't see him, I knew he was sweating heavily. 'That's just about the nicest thing you've ever said to me.'

'Up yours.'

The Colonel didn't bother swapping more compliments; he needed to catch his breath.

And, in all honesty, I wasn't up for it any more. I'd scored my point on the new scummer and was ready to move on.

Instead, I kept my forehead pressed into the lino, smelling

the disinfectant that Ronnie had spread everywhere before the rest of the kids woke up. You can take a man out of the army, but you can't take the army out of a man (his words, not mine).

No, I just lay there, regretting my mistake.

I should have realized that of all the carers in the home, Ronnie was the one who would bother checking I was in my bed last night.

The others never bother. Once we're in our rooms, they're happy to crack on with their game of chess from the last sleepover, or get stuck into the bottle of wine that they'd smuggled in.

But not Ronnie. Nothing went unnoticed on his shift. Everything was run with precision, exactly the way he was taught in the barracks.

A place for everything and everything in its place.

This is the man who would set the table for tomorrow's breakfast while we were swallowing the last mouthful of our dinner, as it saved him minutes the following morning. Yeah, I know, very homely.

He was the Colonel, a legend in his own lunchtime, hated by all, staff included.

And the sad thing was, he was the closest thing I had to a parent.

'If you've calmed down, Billy, I'm prepared to let go,' Ronnie wheezed. 'But if you're still going to display such aggression, then we'll have to sit here a while longer.'

'I'm not the one sitting on a fourteen-year-old's back, so who's the one being aggressive? I don't think it's me, scum.'

He laid on a dramatic sigh.

'Billy, I don't know how many times we have to go over this, my friend. I don't derive any pleasure from this. The reason you are being restrained is simple. You were posing a threat. To the other kids, to me and the other carers, and most importantly to yourself. You walked in that door, after absconding for twelve hours, full of anger. All we did was ask where you'd been. I hardly think that's a reason for throwing a glass at me. We've been worried about you.'

Only cos I ran on your shift, I thought to myself.

It never looked good to those in the office to hear that one of the residents had bolted on your watch. Least of all me.

Didn't earn you any brownie points, that one.

'Well, I'm back now, aren't I? Back to spread a little bit of happiness before you piss off for the day.'

'Oh, I won't be leaving any time soon. Your disappearing has caused me a whole load of paperwork. I've the police to contact, your social worker. Then there's this restraint to write up. And if you hadn't forgotten, it's your case review on Friday. It's my job to try and get you settled somewhere permanent again. Not easy to do, my friend, not easy at all.'

The rest of my fight slipped away as Ronnie mentioned the dreaded 'R' word.

Review.

The most hated day in any lifer's year.

A chance to be lied to by a room full of strangers.

An opportunity to have your life mapped out for you by people who were only there because they were paid to be.

Like the rest of life in care, it was a joke. A bad one.

'Well, if you'd stop bending my arm up my back, you

7

could get started. The report's bound to take you a while. I'm sure you can't rush a good piece of fiction.'

Ronnie sighed again, bigging up the theatrics.

'Billy, it will be just like any of the other *many* restraint reports I've written about you. It will be countersigned by Pete here, to ensure it's accurate –' Mr Uni Graduate nodded wisely – 'and you are welcome to read it, like anything else in your file, if you'd like to make an appointment.'

Then, with a final twist, Ronnie released my arm and stepped away, quickly enough, I noted, to avoid any last-minute lunges.

As if I'd waste my breath.

'Can't say I'll be rushing to have a read, Ronald.' I winced, rubbing at my collarbone. 'Perhaps I'll wait till it's published, eh?'

Point made, I headed for the stairs and the safety of my room.

They reckon a bedroom is important to a kid in care. So my social worker told me anyway.

Meant to be a haven, or some such cack. Somewhere that's yours and yours alone.

Didn't seem to work much like that for me. Mine was a collage of boarded-up windows (the aftermath of Ronnie getting in my face again), stained carpets (yacking after a misadvised bottle of voddy) and a rather sad-looking mattress covered in clothes that were slowly rotting into the duvet.

I didn't even have a wardrobe. Ronnie removed that after I tried to barricade the door a while back.

No, it certainly wasn't a haven, but at least I didn't have

to share, like I heard they do in some other homes. Can you imagine? Waking every night to some snotty little git snivelling for his mummy? I'd rather be on remand.

Slamming the door behind me (just to remind him I was still here), I kicked a pile of festering clothes in front of it (the closest I had to a decent lock) and lay on my mattress, staring at the plastic stars that littered the ceiling.

They must have glowed in the dark once, probably the brainchild of some dumbass social-work scummer, but now they were just shabby and faded, serving no purpose but to give my eyes something to land on.

My arm was sore. But, to be honest, everything aches after a restraint. Not just your muscles either, your brain, your guts, everything. It's difficult to explain. You feel lopsided, out of kilter, just wrong.

I grimaced as I thought back to waking up this morning.

Even though it was the riskiest night's sleep I'd probably ever had, it was also the best I could remember.

Sleep is always fitful. Sometimes because I'm drunk, sometimes because of the twins. But there's always a reason for a broken night.

Not last night.

Last night passed in a flash.

No dreams, no rolling about.

Just eight hours of blissful kip.

I swear I woke up smiling, and that wasn't just to do with where I was.

It was because I'd slept and so I didn't have to think.

No real surprise, I suppose, that the rest of the morning had gone downhill.

Leaving Jan and Grant's had been easy. I just made the bed and let myself out the back door. Didn't want to take the mick by making myself breakfast or nothing. After all, if it had worked once, then a repeat performance wouldn't be out of the question, would it?

No, I just slipped out through the back garden, into the tenfoot at the back, and wandered home.

Maybe I should've given a bit of thought to where I'd been, or tried to sneak in through the fire escape. It wouldn't have been the first time.

I certainly should've realized that Ronnie was on an overnighter and that he'd be looking for any reason to put me on the floor.

That's the thing with him. He has to push. Has to ask the questions. Always expects you to behave like one of his own. Eight years on and he hasn't figured out it doesn't work like that.

Those aren't the rules. Parents don't knock off after a shift.

Carers do. Scummers do.

I can't.

I'm here.

Always have been. Guess I always will.

CHAPTER 2

Have you ever stared at a line of words for so long that they don't make sense any more?

Well, it was happening to me.

I'd been sat in the scummers' study for at least half an hour, looking at the piece of paper that Ronnie had put in front of me.

The questions on it weren't difficult to get my head around or anything.

They were just three easy questions.

The same questions he put in front of me before each of my reviews. All right, he'd dressed up the language as I'd got older, but they were basically the same every year.

'Listen, Bill. This is *your* review, don't forget. It's all well and good me putting a load of legwork into it, but without knowing what you want, how can I possibly go and get it for you?'

I'd heard it all before, and as a result knew he wasn't going to let me leave the room without writing something down. That was what he was like. A twat of the highest order.

I read the first question again.

1. What do you feel are your priorities for the coming year?

I raised my eyebrows and sucked on the pen, nothing coming to mind. Well, nothing that would please him anyway. So I opted for taking the mick.

Finally hatching an escape plan that works. Digging a tunnel big enough for both me and the twins won't be easy, but if I prioritize, a year should be enough time.

I nodded my approval as I read it back. Yep, made sense to me, so I moved on to number two.

2. How can your key worker, carers and social worker help you achieve this goal?

Simple, that one, so I put pen to paper.

Keeping me stocked up with spades would help. And if they could clear away the rubble from the tunnels, that would definitely speed up the process.

Number three hardly tested me either.

3. Where would you like to be in a year's time?

I scribbled the answer down without thinking.

ANYWHERE BUT HERE.

Satisfied that my work was done, I jammed the lid back on the pen and turned to Ronnie, who was scribbling away at the other desk, open files scattered around him.

'I'm done,' I muttered, avoiding eye contact of any kind.

'And have you written anything?'

'Oh aye, more than ever.' Which, strictly speaking, wasn't a lie.

'Where are you off to now?'

'Out.'

'Where to?'

'Somewhere.'

'And when will you be back?'

'When I'm finished,' I huffed, although by that point I knew I was out of earshot and through the front door.

Leaving the house is something I do a lot. Sometimes because I'm hacked off, sometimes because I'm up to no good, and sometimes just because it creates work for the scummers.

That's one of the things about living in a kids' home. Everything you do creates work for the scum. It is a magnificent way of messing with their heads and adding more to their plates.

If I break a window, there's an incident report to write. If I whack one of the other scummers, there's another. But here's the best thing. If I even leave the house, they have to write it down.

The house has a logbook, you see, and it's supposed to monitor where each of us is at any time. Where we are, what we've eaten and how much, what time we were up, what time we went to sleep. And whenever we leave.

I don't know if we're supposed to know about it.

I don't know if the other lifers even care.

But me?

I love it.

Use it to my advantage every time I can.

On average I must go through the front door at least twenty times a day, not including when I actually need to. Gives me a bit of joy, it does, to see them scampering to the office, biro in hand, every time I step off the front porch.

I always make sure I'm outside for at least ten minutes,

though. Some of the older scummers think they're wise to it, you see. Reckon I'll be back in seconds, but when I'm not, and they know they've got the senior scum in head office checking procedure all the time, they've got no option but to log it.

Brilliant, eh? Makes the long repetitive days just fly by.

After wasting half an hour in front of Ronnie's pointless questions, though, I was in need of some air and tried to chill out in the garden.

Not that there was much chance of that happening. Not with other lifers getting in your face.

Don't get me wrong, there have been times when I've made friends with other kids here. Or alliances at least.

But not for a long time.

I mean, what's the point?

People move on. Quickly as well. I've gone to bed some nights and found rooms empty the next morning. And not just once or twice. It happens all the time.

So now I don't bother trying to get to know people. And I certainly don't tell them anything. Except not to mess with me.

Unfortunately, some people don't get to grips with that quickly enough. So I have to remind them.

Charlie Windass was one of those kids. He'd been with us months, and was only a year younger than me, so he should've known better than to get in my face.

'Hey, Bill,' he crowed, marching over to where I was sat. 'I hear you've got your review this week.'

I tried to ignore him, but when he kicked the toe of his trainer against mine and repeated the question, I knew it wasn't an option.

'Didn't you hear me?'

'Yeah, I heard you. I just don't want to talk to you.'

He tried to look hurt, but he just looked pathetic.

'Well, that's not very brotherly of you, is it? I'm only trying to talk to you.'

I bristled at the suggestion of him being family.

'Listen, mate,' I growled. 'I don't know who sent you over here, or whether you've got a death wish or something, but let's get something straight, shall we? I'm not your brother, right? We may sleep under the same roof, but you aren't, and never will be, a friend. I don't want to talk to you. I don't even want to look at you. So get out of my face, all right?'

I saw a hint of a smile on his face and knew instantly he was after a ruck. Which was fine by me.

'Jesus, they're right about you, aren't they?' He laughed. 'Soon as I arrived the others told me you were a loon. And they were right. No wonder you and the other two have been here since you were born.'

And that was it. Game on.

Charlie may have been in care a while, but his skills didn't match the speed of his mouth. I don't know if he was expecting a fair fight or something, but he certainly didn't protect himself, and a swift kick to the nads saw him on the floor.

To his credit, he tried his best to even things up, but his kick at the back of my knee was just lame and left me no option but to make my point more forcefully.

Pinning his arms with my knees and sitting on his waist to disable his legs, I leaned over him, spitting angrily while backhanding him several times a sentence.

15

'What the others should have told you, Charlie, is that being a loon makes me the sort of person you should avoid. Not mess with. You get me?'

I pressed my palm against the end of his nose and forced it back towards his eyes. I saw his tears, but he remained silent. So I pressed harder.

I don't know how much longer he'd have stayed quiet, or how much further I'd have pushed, because I felt two arms grip me by my shoulders, pulling me backwards.

By that point I was too far into the zone to think clearly about what was happening and I lashed out wildly with my fists, happy to fight the whole world. No one was going to take me down in this mood.

Apart from three scummers, that is.

They must have been watching from the window or something, because they were there so quick, two of them taking an arm each, while the Colonel wrapped his arms around my legs and hung on like a rodeo rider.

I bucked and wriggled as they carried me back towards the house, but they were just too strong to break away from, and too far out of range to land a decent throatful of spit on.

By the time we reached the house, I knew the game was up, but I was still too angry to quit. Especially as Charlie Windass was back on his feet, flashing the wanker sign at me as he stumbled after us.

I tried to calm myself with the thought that he'd keep. There was plenty of time to get my revenge. We were lifers, after all.

CHAPTER 3

I struggle with school.

Not with the learning bit. If I chose to go, I'd learn. I'm not thick.

What I can't get my head around is the idea of a job at the end of it.

I mean, it doesn't matter if I know where a comma goes, or what the capital of Spain is. Any boss seeing me walk in for an interview is more likely to call security than to offer me a gig. Fact.

I'm not looking for sympathy. I've seen it. Time and time again. You don't live here this long without learning. Unfortunately, what I've learned doesn't give you the tools to earn a tenner an hour.

Take Marie.

Classic example.

Lived here six years, from twelve till they packed her off at eighteen.

Marie was pretty straight. Wasn't into any particular scene. Wasn't really a drinker or a smoker. Went to school. Don't think I ever saw her restrained. Not even as a result of me or one of the other lifers acting out.

Course, as soon as she turned seventeen, they started prepping her for leaving. Getting her own gaff, nice place too.

'You should see it, Bill,' she raved. 'Brand spanking new flat on that development by the old town. Council place, but still tidy.'

Life skills, they called them. Everything she'd need to know to live on her own.

But nothing could prepare her. Not after living here six years.

On the day she turned eighteen, she packed her bags and was off, and at first it all seemed rosy. The flat was fine, she kept in touch with her social worker, seemed to be coping with the life skills rubbish.

Except she couldn't get a job. At first she set her sights high. Office junior at some company in town. She thought the interview went well, thought she'd answered all the questions, reckoned she was in.

But she wasn't. They turned her down.

And so did everyone else. Betting shops, Blockbuster, nurseries, pubs. They all saw something that didn't add up, didn't appeal.

Before she knew it, she had bills. Loads of them. And the life skills couldn't pay them. And neither could all the school lessons she'd sat in like some obedient puppy.

So Marie did what any lifer would do. She arsed it up completely.

Started delivering for some guy who lived in her block.

'I'm not daft,' she told me. 'I know what it is I'm carrying. And that's all it is, a bit of fetch and carry for a mate.'

I didn't buy into that. Marie was just like me, and I know I couldn't resist a quick dabble on whatever it was in that bag.

Something got the better of her anyhow. Last time I was round her flat you could barely get in the door for the bills wedged behind it.

'Don't be soft, Bill,' she said to me, when I asked if she'd given in to temptation. 'Just isn't my thing. My mum's maybe, but not mine.'

To be honest, that was the last time I spoke to Marie. The lure of going to her gaff to escape the Colonel lost its appeal. It was in a right state. After a few months she'd flogged the TV, the stereo, all the good stuff. Made my room look like the Ritz.

From what I heard, though, things went downhill pretty quickly.

She started skimming off the packages she was meant to be delivering. Naturally the dealer got wise and wanted paying back.

Not money, you understand, something a bit more intimate, and not just for him. For his boys as well.

I don't have to spell it out, do I? Last anyone saw of Marie, she was standing by the industrial site round the back of the cinema, all blank eyes and pincushion arms.

Well, bugger that. And bugger school as well if that's where it gets you.

Mind you, endless days in the home weren't any better. Especially as Ronnie had all the scummers well briefed on what my day should involve.

Each morning they'd go through the routine of setting

up a desk for me in the kitchen, the same work from the day before that I'd refused to look at. The same pencil sat by it, which was always blunt. I meant to ask if that was intentional.

I mean, I'm not a savage. If it's going to go off, I've got my fists; I don't need a sharpened HB.

I always sit at the desk, just to give them that bit of hope, before swinging on the chair, tapping the pencil on my teeth and trying to get to the kettle to make a brew before they stop me. As soon as they get a bit lairy, I'll tip the table over, or rip up the book, or snap the pencil. Whatever takes my fancy. Whatever gets the message across that the work thing isn't going to happen.

The problem with this is that it makes for a pretty dull day. All the others are at school, all nine of them.

The twins included.

I make them go. No messing. Because the difference is we won't be here much longer. We'll be rehoused, sorted, and then school will mean something for them. Be important. Bigger picture and all that.

So when the table's gone over by nine thirty, it means I've got another six hours until they get home. That's a fair wedge of time to fill.

Especially when the Colonel's locked the door to the TV room.

'Billy, if you want to watch the box, you earn it, sunshine.' It was always the same line. The same wind-up. The same restraint. The same arm up my back. Even the tussle became a bit dull after a while.

So I spent the majority of days in my room. Staring at the

20

plastic stars. Wondering what it would take to get them shining again. Either that or dreaming of ways to run rings round the Colonel.

I swear that once the clock hits three, it slows down, goes to double time or something. Like it's another way of punishing me.

I'm always desperate to get out the door and meet them at the gates, but the Colonel has put that to bed.

'Sounds like a privilege to me, Bill. Once you're back at school or engaging with work from home, then we can look at it again. Until then, during school hours, the outside world is off limits.'

Man, I'd like to hurt him.

But instead all I can do is invent new ways to get at him, idling away the minutes until the door bursts open and the twins get home.

They'll be ten this year, and it kills me that this is all they've known. They don't remember what it is to be home, to not have a daily routine that runs like a military operation.

All they have is me, and that's what worries me.

The house practically shuddered as the door was flung back on its hinges. The hurricane hit and, as always, I was ready for it as its full force slammed into my chest.

'Biiiilll,' Lizzie shouted, and the words rang in my left ear as Louie, true to form, bellowed the same into my right.

'Now then, troubles.' I beamed as I gave them the once-over. 'How was your day?'

'All right,' they groaned. 'Same as always.'

'Anyone give you any grief?'

'Not today. Well, only Ronnie for not having my tie on

when I came out of school,' moaned Louie, with a smile. 'So I told him where to go.'

'Oi, oi. You leave that to me. You just keep your head down and do as he tells you, you hear?'

'I hear you.'

'Right. Well, get up the stairs, both of you, and get yourselves changed. Then we'll find ourselves something to do before tea.'

As they slumped upstairs, I noticed Ronnie behind me in the doorway.

'You really *are* good with them, you know,' he said, a smile on his face.

'What do you expect?' I replied, as I hung their coats on their pegs. Ten pegs and ten names in black marker pen. Classy, eh?

'I just wonder how you can be so different with them to everyone else you live with.' As if it's a big surprise. 'It's like watching a different person.'

'Because I live with *them* by choice. I can hardly say that about the rest of you, can I?'

And besides, I thought, *you* don't live here. None of you scummers do. We just pay your wages. Biting my lip, I followed them up the stairs. I couldn't be arsed to get into it again.

'Are you eating with the rest of us tonight? I thought I might stay and eat before getting off . . .' He stopped himself before finishing with the word 'home'.

But I knew what he was going to say, so I chose to ignore him.

*

The rest of the day passed off the same as most. It's all about routine for the scummers. Makes their shift end quicker and easier, and gets them to the pub on time.

But it does nothing for me or the twins.

The rest of the lifers can do what they say, but not us. So while the rest of them crowded round the board to see what was for dinner, I was in the larder with the twins, choosing what we were going to cook.

None of the other lifers question it any more, only the new scummers that seem to start work in the house every other week. All the others know the score.

Me and the twins fend for ourselves. Choose what we're having between us, not mapped out in advance by Ronnie.

'Make sure you tidy any mess up,' said the Colonel from the doorway.

I can tell that it still gets to him, no matter how much he tries to hide it, but this is one thing I don't do to wind him up. It's about trying to do something normal. Or what I'm guessing normal is.

Once the conveyor belt of dinner was over, the other lifers piled into the lounge for their dose of TV before Operation Bedtime begins, the most stressful part of any scummer's shift. It's hardly fun for the lifers either. I still see it in the twins, despite being here so long.

'You are going to read to us tonight, aren't you, Bill?' asked Lizzie.

'After your bath I will,' I replied, waiting for the next question.

'And you will wait outside the bathroom while I'm in there, won't you?'

23

'If that's what you want, yeah.'

'The others are always trying the door while I'm in there. I don't like it.'

'I know you don't, Lizzie. But there's no need to worry. Anyone coming near the door will get a dig from me, all right?'

And that seemed to help a bit.

But it's the same anxiety every night as bedtime approaches. Hardly surprising when you're faced with being put to bed by scummers who are practically strangers.

No one puts the twins to bed but me.

And they won't have it any other way.

I don't know how they managed when I was living at Jan and Grant's.

I was a mess.

When bedtime came around, I'd sit in my posh new room and try to remember who would be on shift that night. But even if it was one of the better scummers, I still wanted to run back to them, screaming that I was on the way, not to worry.

I never did run back there, though. Well, I did at first, but the scummers would never let me past the front gate. And when things got a bit lairy, it was never long before they called the rozzers, who'd drag me home, much to Jan and Grant's delight.

I had to make do with nightly phone calls, followed by hours worrying myself sick.

About someone different tucking them in every night. Not knowing what stories to read and in what order. Not knowing to tuck the duvet in under their feet to keep them warm. Not sitting in the doorway until they nodded off.

Killed me, it did.

Still does.

So now I make sure that, whatever's gone on in the day, I'm here for bedtime.

Sitting in the doorway, listening to their breathing deepen, I could feel the knot tightening inside me.

As the crying started down the hallway and the yells for mummy pealed off the walls, I knew it was going to be another typical night in hell.

Another night sitting and counting the stars in my room, thinking about escaping, thinking about screaming myself, thinking I'm about to lose the plot.

CHAPTER 4

The chair groaned as I pushed back on to two legs, forcing me to make eye contact with the rest of the room. Quite a turnout, it was. In fact, never in my long and illustrious career as Billy Finn, professional lifer, had I seen such a collection of scummers.

The Colonel was there of course, shoes glistening and shirt pressed. I was almost surprised he hadn't buffed up his medals and pinned them to his chest as well, then he'd really have been ready for inspection.

Tony, the fat controller who ran the home, was there too, though how they squeezed him into his chair was beyond me. Must have poured him into a mould, I decided, grinning inwardly.

Then there was Dawn, my social worker of the month. A decent sort. Kind, caring, thoughtful. Everything a social worker shouldn't be. Still, she was young. She'd learn. Either that or have a breakdown within six months. She wouldn't be the first, believe me.

The other bod in the room I didn't recognize, or trust for that matter. He stank of social work. Covered in corduroy and spectacles. Except he didn't smell of fear, like Dawn. He had a calm about him, as if he knew why he was here. And that bothered me.

He clocked me, gave me a smile, and nodded to Dawn to get the ball rolling.

'Right, shall we start?' she cooed, like she was about to run a game of bingo rather than sounding the bell for round one. Made me think this was probably her first case-review meeting.

'Let me introduce everyone to you, Billy. Obviously, you know me, Ronald and . . . er, Tony,' she added, checking her notes nervously. 'But this is Christopher, head of childcare services for the borough. Given your age, and the, um, challenges we face in finding you some stability and forming a comprehensive new care plan, we thought Christopher's input would be invaluable today.'

'Very nice to meet you, Billy. I've been reading your file at length.'

I bet you have, I thought to myself. You could have *built* me and the twins a house to live in from all the files on me.

'But I thought it might be more useful if you gave me an idea of your background. I can only learn so much from this,' he said, gesturing at a bulging A4 file.

Silence.

If he thought he was getting the life story from me, he was mistaken.

But if the quiet bothered him, he certainly didn't show it. He just sat there looking at me. I don't think he even blinked for the first minute.

The others were getting twitchy. I could see it. Tony was tapping his teeth with his biro. Dawn was flicking through her notes as if that was going to help her. If it was answers she was after, she wasn't going to find any in the pages of my file.

It was certainly too much for Ronnie. Sweat was already pooling on his top lip and his leg was twitching against the table, causing the teacups to shudder.

'It's over eight years now since Billy first came to live with us,' he barked suddenly. 'It was just after his sixth birthday. The twins came at the same time, obviously. Life at home had been very unstable. Mum and her boyfriend, Shaun, who is the twins' father but not Billy's, had alcohol and substance issues, and there were obvious indications of both emotional and physical abuse.'

I felt my pulse quicken for a minute at the mention of his name, but tried to breathe through it.

Keep cool. Keep cool.

'Hmmm,' said Christopher, with a chin stroke added for dramatic effect. You'd have thought someone had just explained the secret of eternal youth to him, not read out my admissions report. 'You must know this house inside out by now.'

I smiled my falsest smile.

More than you could ever know, pal. But that doesn't mean I'm going to talk to you.

'Tell me, Billy,' he asked, leaning forward. 'How is that for you? For the three of you of course, but in particular for you? I'd imagine the twins' memory of arriving here is sketchy at best.'

'S'like Disney World,' I mumbled.

'I'm sorry?' he asked, leaning further still.

'I SAID –' cupping my hand around my mouth like a foghorn – 's'like Disney World. Everywhere I look I see Mickey Mouse.'

I could feel Ronnie stiffen beside me. Perfect.

Christopher, though, looked unflustered, as relaxed as before. In fact, he even allowed himself a sympathetic smile.

'No, I can imagine it must be incredibly difficult for you. To be so long in one place. Although I did notice,' he said, flicking through the file, 'that you had a placement outside of the home for a period.' And again he leaned forward, inviting a response.

Bollocks. First Shaun and now this.

I didn't like where it was going and I dropped my eyes for the first time, which I realized instantly was a mistake. He knew he'd hit on something, and if he was like the other scummers I'd met, he wasn't going to move on until he was ready.

I tried to hold on to the silence that I'd started with, focusing on the coffee cup still gently shaking on the table. Until I noticed it wasn't Ronnie's leg making it quiver any more. It was mine, and that was too much.

'What is it you're trying to get at? I don't see what it is you're trying to get out of me here.'

'All I'm trying to do, Billy, is understand you. Because if I don't understand what has happened to you over the years, then how can we sit here and work out what's best for you going forward?'

Typical social-work cack, but I knew there was more to come, and the sooner he spouted it, the sooner I'd be out of there.

Christopher turned his eyes back to my file. I knew what was coming.

'I see that you spent six months with a family, Billy. How long ago was that?'

'Three years ago now,' interrupted Ronnie.

It was almost a relief to see someone as on edge as me, but for different reasons. He was just ticking down the seconds until he had to put my arm up my back again. He knew he was the only one in the room capable of stopping me from ripping Christopher's throat out.

'It's incredibly rare, you know, Billy, to find a placement at the age of eleven. People looking to foster, or in the case of . . .' He paused as his eyes flicked back to the file.

'Jan and Grant,' I muttered. *Why was I helping him?*

'Thank you, yes, the Scotts. I see here that it wasn't just a fostering placement they were offering you. They were *adopting* you. I can't begin to tell you how rare that is. You know that, don't you, Billy?'

I shrugged, as if it was news to me.

'So what happened? I need to understand, when you were offered the chance that so many children like you dream of, why or how it could go so wrong.'

As he spoke, and dug away at me, at stuff that no one dared to go near, I could feel a knot building in my stomach, and as it built I could feel it bumping the anger that sat above it ever closer to the surface.

'Why are you asking me? Don't you think you're asking the wrong person here? You should be asking them, Jan and Grant. They're the ones who sent me back. I didn't leave. They didn't WANT me.'

'But, Billy, you have to understand your part in this. These people *did* want you. Wanted you to be their son, not for a year, not until you turned eighteen, but for the rest of your life. But you made their lives impossible. You smashed windows, you disappeared for days on end. You know what else you did, don't you? I don't want to go over the other incidents. I'm not here to provoke you, I'm here to move things on.'

The rage was in my throat now. It was impossible to speak. He'd gone too far and he knew it, so Dawn stepped in.

'What worries us, Billy, what worries all of us here is that we can see you repeating yourself again. The absconding, the vandalism, your non-attendance at school. All behaviours you exhibited towards the end of your stay with the Scotts. And no one here wants to see the same incidents unfold again.'

'Do you realize how many times we've had to restrain you in the last two months, Bill?' Tony chipped in. 'Fourteen times. Twice in the last three days! And it's not like you're eight years old any more. You'll soon be fifteen. Do you realize how hard it is for the staff to go through that week after week?'

'Then back off and leave me alone,' I spat. 'Every time they put me on the floor, it's because they don't know how to leave well enough alone.'

'Come on, Billy, that's simply not true. Your behaviour is completely unpredictable. We never know what's going to trigger the next incident.' Ronnie looked almost believable.

'What Tony is saying, in a roundabout way,' interrupted

Christopher, 'is that you are standing at a crossroads here, Billy. The current state of affairs simply can't continue, for Ronnie, for the other carers and residents, and for you.'

'We just can't cope with you in the same way any more, Billy. We're just not equipped to give you what you need.'

The knot inside me turned into a fist and started jabbing at my stomach. I couldn't believe I'd arrived at this point again.

'Where are you sending me?' I asked.

'We're not sending you anywhere, Bill. Not at the moment. We're offering you one last opportunity to turn yourself around. Cut out the challenging behaviour and attend school. You know what it is you have to do.'

'And if I don't?'

'Then we will have to look at an alternative placement for you. There are some brilliant therapeutic units that could offer you the help you need. The chance to sort out whatever it is that's bothering you.'

'You mean secure units?'

'No, Billy. We're not talking about locking you up. It's not about that. It's about keeping you safe, sorting you out. These places could offer practically one-on-one care, sessions with therapists, and there'd be fewer kids living there, so fewer distractions.'

'But what about the twins? I don't see how that would help them. They don't need therapy. They're nine years old.'

Christopher shook his head. 'No, Billy. Let's get one thing straight. This placement would be just for you. It wouldn't involve the twins.'

Too much, too much, and before I knew it I was on my feet.

'Hang on a minute here. You can't split us up. They need me, they do. I'm all they've got.'

'I appreciate that, Billy. But have you stopped to consider the twins in all this? How do you think they feel when they see you so angry all the time?'

'They know the score. They can see Ronnie keeps setting me up. He tries to do the same to them, for God's sake!'

'I'm sorry, Billy, but that's just not true. Ron has only their best interests at heart, just as he does for you. What you have to try and understand is that the only bad influence around the twins, the only danger around them, in all honesty, is *you*.'

The dam burst at his words, and before I knew it, I'd launched myself across the table, scattering the teacups in all directions.

I didn't reach Christopher, however, as Ronnie and Tony flew from their chairs, grabbing a leg each, before pinning me on the table. So that's why Tony was really there. Backup. Hired muscle.

Lifting my head, I caught a glimpse of fear on Christopher's face for the first time. For the first time he'd seen the real me. Knew what I was all about. Knew what I was capable of.

I could read what his eyes were saying.

I'm not surprised they gave you up. I'm not surprised they sent you back.

That made two of us.

CHAPTER 5

I've never been much good under pressure, and the weeks following the review were no exception, especially as school decided they wouldn't be ready for me to return for at least a month. Apparently they needed time to plan my 'integration', which I knew was a lie.

They just didn't want me there. Either that or the teachers were demanding extra training to cope. Or more money.

Either way, it didn't help me.

Now they had me over a barrel, I knew I had to at least look willing, and it's easier to do that in a room of thirty kids than sat on your own in the kitchen with the Colonel watching you like a hawk. Every minute was shocking and, to be honest, I hadn't a clue what the textbooks were on about most of the time. I'd missed too much to catch up without someone explaining everything to me like a toddler.

So I just tried to copy as much from the textbooks as I could and used the limited time I had with a computer to download stuff.

It was so dull, although the Colonel had such low expectations of me that I didn't worry about getting anything right. I doubted he'd even look at it. As long as I was quiet and he didn't have to sit on me, I reckoned he might give me some space.

I just wished he'd leave the twins alone.

Now I was working during the day, he had no option but to let me join him in picking them up from school, and my God he was a pain in the arse.

They'd come screaming out the gates like any of the other kids, full of joy at finishing for the day. But within seconds he'd knock the stuffing right out of them. If they didn't have their tie on they'd get the third degree, or if their jumper was round their waist you'd think the world had ended. The man was obsessed.

But what could I do? I just had to sit there and simmer.

And I could see he loved every minute of it. He knew he could wind me up and there was nothing I could do, except kick off. And I wasn't going to give him what he wanted.

I never had and I wasn't going to start now.

I just ploughed every bit of energy I had into the twins. They didn't have a clue what was going on, and I certainly wasn't going to tell them. They'd been there before. I'd seen how gutted they were when I went to Jan and Grant's; there was no way I was putting them through that again.

There were so many nights when they'd called me before they went to bed, and although they never actually cried down the phone, I could hear the fear in their voices. Knew that once the call was over and they were left alone in their room the tears would follow. Killed me, it did, made me feel so guilty, like I had abandoned them, just as Annie had.

No, it had to be business as usual, and that included getting them ready for contact.

Saturday afternoon was contact time. Had been for as long as I could remember, and, as always, the twins were bouncing off the walls with excitement.

'Where do you think Mum'll take us, Bill?' asked Louie.

'The cinema. She promised last week.' Lizzie was in no doubt, and I didn't have the heart to put her right. Annie had a shortlist of places to take the twins. All of them were cheap and none of them the cinema.

But at least she was turning up now. There had been periods in the early days when she didn't appear for months on end. And there were never any apologies. We were lucky if she remembered birthdays. Not that the twins noticed. I became pretty good at forging her signature on cards.

'Why don't you come with us today, Bill?' asked Louie. 'Mum won't mind. She'd love to take us all out.'

My heart sank, as it always did. They didn't understand, and why would they? How do you explain to your brother and sister that your mother doesn't want *you* any more? That she's only interested in them.

'Look, Louie. You only have two hours a week with Annie. You don't need me in the way. Besides, I'm not really bothered about the cinema. Get out there and have fun. I'll be here when you get back.'

Louie shrugged it off, as he always did, and started kicking the wall with excitement.

Annie arrived on time again, looking smarter than usual. Maybe she'd bought her clothes somewhere other than a car boot sale. She even tried to strike up a conversation.

'So, how's it going, then, Bill? I hear you'll be back at school soon. That's great news.'

I forced a smile, for the twins. 'Yeah, in a few weeks. Should be all right.'

'It'll be more than that. It's important you get some exams. Don't make the same mistakes I did.'

I swallowed my disgust. *What, choose some alcoholic loser over your kids?* Wasn't high on my list of priorities, to be honest.

'Where are we going today, Mum?' shouted Lizzie, dizzy with excitement.

'Can't you remember, chuckie?' Annie laughed, her throat thick with ciggie smoke.

'CINEMA!' roared the twins together.

'That's right. A promise is a promise, and I've been looking forward to it all week.'

At that moment, Ronnie appeared in the doorway, pulling on his jacket as he greeted Annie, all pats on the head for the twins. I backed away, worried he might try to show some affection towards me.

'Right then, kids. Are we all ready?' he boomed, striding down the steps and towards the car park.

Louie seemed hesitant for a second, throwing me a worried look before jumping on me for a hug.

'See you later, big man,' I said, forcing a grin. 'Have a wicked time. Save me some pick 'n' mix!'

'No way, fatty!' He laughed as he pulled away, leaving a hole that couldn't be filled.

Lizzie was already halfway to the car, still spinning around on Annie's outstretched arm.

'Shit,' I whispered to myself.

As they walked off, the four of them, they looked too much like a family to me.

I didn't like it. Annie was getting herself together, doing a decent impression of a proper mother. This wasn't good. It wasn't good at all.

The twins didn't want to go to bed when they got back. They were so excited I pretty much had to scrape them off the ceiling. Their heads were full of the cinema and popcorn. Even Ronnie was wearing a smile. That never happened when it was his weekend on.

'You should've seen the special effects, Billy,' Louie whooped. 'They were wicked. Mum reckoned all the explosions were real, and they looked it too, except I knew it was all CGI.'

'And you should've seen the size of the bag of pick 'n' mix Louie got down his neck,' bragged Lizzie.

'I can imagine,' I said, trying for the fifth time to get to the end of the bedtime book.

'Mum said we can go see it again next week. You'll come next week, won't you, Bill? I told Mum you would.'

'We'll see,' I said, smiling as I tucked the duvets under their feet in turn. 'Time to sleep now. I'll see you in the morning.'

As I reached the door, I stopped and waited for the question that always came, every night without fail: 'Sit at the door till we fall asleep, Bill?'

But tonight it never came. Instead they talked excitedly about what they'd seen, what they'd done, what Annie had bought them on the way to the film.

It didn't do much for the mood I'd been in all afternoon.

I hadn't known what to do with myself after the twins left, so I did what I always did. Lay on my back and stared at the ceiling, counting the stars from right to left. From the door to the ceiling and back again. Seventy-three, as always.

I'd fancied getting my hands on some booze, and had I not been on this final warning I would have gone out and cadged some from the offie.

I'm not fussy about what I drink. Beer's fine, but vodka's stronger. And the scum don't smell it on your breath as easily either.

The only thing I won't touch is whisky.

Whisky equals Shaun.

It was always his poison, the drink that really stirred the devil in him. The drink that led him to me. Even the smell of it now is enough to give me the shakes.

Anyway, I steered clear of any booze that afternoon.

Because of the twins. Because of what would happen if they caught me. Of what would happen to them.

So hearing them full of Annie stung me. But I couldn't let it show. She'd let them down before. Not recently, like, but it was only a matter of time before she slipped up again.

So I sat in the doorway as usual and listened to their babbling.

It took them a good hour to talk themselves out. To be honest, I wasn't sure most of the time if they knew I was there. I hoped so, though.

Once they settled, I crept away from their door and closed it with a gentle snick.

The house was pretty quiet for a Saturday night, which

I knew would please the scummers. It was handover time. Ron would be off home to his proper family soon, to his trophy wife and perfect boys, leaving the lifers to the confusion of waking up to different people in the morning.

I slid quietly down the stairs, hoping I could get into the TV room and avoid Ronnie before he left. He was in the study, giving the night shift the lowdown on what had gone on.

But as I tiptoed past I heard Annie mentioned. Had it been anyone else's name I wouldn't have broken my step, but the paranoia in me was still burning up.

'Yeah, I was pretty impressed again.' It was Ron. 'I've known her a long time now, seen her at her worst. In fact, there was a long period in the early days when we didn't see her at all. But it looks to me like she's turned a corner.'

'For how long, though?' asked a sceptical voice. It was Mally, one of the night-shifters. A favourite of mine, never once checked on where I was. 'Haven't we heard and seen it all before?'

'Feels different to me this time, though, Mal.' Ronnie again. 'I know she's been unreliable before, but she's been consistent for the past year now. Just as she said she would be.'

'She's looking to increase the amount of contact with the twins, then?'

I crept closer to the door.

'Yep, should start twice-weekly in the next month, and if that goes well the unsupervised contact will increase as well. It's what we laid out at the last review.'

Was it? It was the first I'd heard of it.

I could almost see the smile on Ronnie's face.

The last thing the twins needed was more broken promises from Annie. The scummers should have been concentrating on finding a proper foster family for the three of us, or moving us to a smaller home. Not dicking around, wasting time on her.

'Annie's adamant this time. Reckons she's finished with all the losers she's shacked up with in the past, and, to be fair, there's been no sign of Shaun for years. That job she's landed seems to have helped as well. It's been a year now since she started. You can see the difference in her.'

'Bit late now, though,' snorted Mally.

He obviously wasn't taken in by Annie. Top man.

'The Finns have lived here eight years. She can't seriously think she can get the twins back after all that time.'

The blood was pounding round my head. I was worried it was affecting my hearing.

I hoped it was.

'It would be unusual, I grant you. But what's the alternative, Mal? The twins will be ten next birthday. It's not easy finding a placement when kids are that old. Especially when there's two of them. Look at what happened to Bill. He was back here within six months.'

Mally sighed. 'It's Billy I worry about. I know the kid's hard work, but the twins are the only thing that keeps him even vaguely straight. Send them back to Annie and he'll lose it. Unless she takes the three of them back.'

'It's not that easy, though, is it?' said Ronnie, without hesitating. 'She gave Billy up for adoption when the Scotts offered him a permanent placement. Legally I think it would

41

be tricky to reverse that. Besides, could she cope with the three of them? I reckon we have to focus on the twins and getting them home. It's too late for Billy on that score.'

I couldn't believe what I was hearing. I wanted to rip his head off. They'd been planning this for months, knowing that they wanted to take the twins away from me and send them back to her. It took everything I had to stop myself from kicking the door in and jumping him.

I had to think. Clear my head, or break someone else's. But I knew I couldn't do either here. That wouldn't help me or the twins. So I bolted for the front door and out into the night.

CHAPTER 6

I wish I could tell you that it felt better to be out walking the streets, but it didn't. I couldn't make sense of what I'd heard. Couldn't get over the fact that the Colonel had been planning it all behind my back.

As well as being angry at him, I was just as furious with myself for not seeing through it earlier. All that crap that they spouted at my review about giving me one more chance, about changing my behaviour for the sake of the twins and staying together. It was all cack. Filthy scummer lies.

Usually, when I'm this hacked off, night-walking helps.

Mostly because there's no one around and you can get away with more.

Don't get the wrong idea. I'm not one of those kids who walks around with a spray can, getting all arty on the side of a bus, or even those who scratch their names into the wall with a compass. I'm not creative, and I certainly don't want the scummers seeing where I've been.

No, if I've got the taste for it, I'll just look for a decent car to key, or a window to put through. There's nothing artistic in it; it just makes me feel better. Lifts the clouds for a minute or two. Enough time to catch a glimpse of the stars.

Nothing was hitting the spot tonight, though. There wasn't a window big enough to get rid of the angry knot in my gut, and believe me I tried a few. Even if I painted a picture of Ronnie's face on it first. Before smashing it with a single punch.

I'm reasonably handy with my fists.

You wouldn't last five minutes as a lifer if you weren't, never mind eight years.

It's rare for a day to pass by in our house without it kicking off. More often than not, the rucks start at breakfast when someone finishes the cereal that someone else was after. You know, the serious stuff in life.

It's pretty obvious why fights flare up first thing. As soon as I open my eyes and realize I'm still in Oldfield House, I feel pretty angry. Wouldn't you?

So when you chuck nine or ten kids, all feeling gnarly, into the same room, well, you don't have to be smart to work it out, do you?

The scummers can't get their heads around it, and Ronnie didn't go for my idea of serving everyone breakfast in bed.

'You wouldn't get that at home every day, Bill, so it doesn't happen here. We're a family. And families eat together.'

Yeah, whatever. Strangely, I don't remember family members wrestling each other over the dregs of the Coco Pops. I must have had a lie-in at home that day.

Of course the other lifers know better than to get in my way first thing.

Or the twins' way, for that matter. In fact, not just at breakfast. At any time of day. They know it doesn't take much to earn a dig or two.

My ability to deliver a clean right has always bothered the Colonel. So much so that he reckoned at one point that boxing might just be the answer. What was he basing this on? The army of course.

'We had a number of lads who struggled with discipline. The first thing we did was get them in the ring. Gave them a focus for all that aggression.'

I wasn't impressed.

'So what do you think, Bill?' he asked.

'To what?'

'To giving it a go. Boxing.'

'Who would I be fighting?'

'Don't know. Other lads your age. Older lads as well if you're any good.'

'I wouldn't be sparring with you?'

'No, of course not.'

'Think I'll give it a miss, then.'

Honestly. He'd been watching too many films. If he really thought I was going to have some change of heart and discover myself by pulling on a pair of boxing gloves, then he'd taken too many punches himself.

Did he actually think I enjoyed kicking off? If he thought about it properly he'd realize the only reason I think with my fists is because of the way he treats me. The way he tries to plan my life.

When all I am to him is a job.

It's not as if I really matter to him, not like his real kids do. He's forever going on about them. The footie teams they've been picked for. The exams they've passed. It feels like I live with them, the amount I hear. Not that he's ever

45

brought them near this place. He wouldn't want his precious boys mixing with the likes of me.

I mean, what would happen if I said yes to the boxing? It'd be like shaking the world's biggest bottle of Coke, then taking the lid off without knowing how you were going to get it back on. Did he really think that I'd stop throwing punches when the bell rang?

There was too much stuff waiting to burst out for that. They'd have to hoist me out of the ring with a crane before I stopped swinging.

In my mind there was only one place that could help me that night. One place where I reckoned my mind would relax even a bit. It had worked the month before and I reckoned it would do the trick again.

I went on to autopilot as I neared the house. Although it was three years since I'd regularly walked the route, it was ingrained in my mind. The quick scoot across the dual carriageway, stopping to kick at the flowers that grew in the central reservation. Then down Garton Ave, a left at the allotments where the local kids, me included, would meet to down whatever we could steal from parents or the offie. Then a final right on to Walton Street, past the dark spot where the first two street lights were still bust. Nothing to do with me either, before you ask.

I stopped and leaned against the second lamp post, daring myself to lift my eyes in the direction of Jan and Grant's.

I knew the next split second would decide my mood for the rest of the night. And I really needed some peace for my head.

I hadn't planned that first trip back there the month before. And I definitely hadn't planned to let myself in like I had.

The autopilot had taken me there. I'd had a rubbish night, as the result of a crappy day. Ronnie and the scummers had pinned me to the floor for dishing out some justice to one of the other lifers, who'd made the mistake of giving Louie some lip. I hadn't gone too far, just a handful of digs to remind him of how things worked. It wasn't as if I'd busted his nose or anything. He just bled easily, that's all.

All the same, I'd spent the next twenty minutes eating carpet thanks to a couple of fifteen-stone scummers. And for some reason, it had got to me. Maybe because Louie had seen me pinned to the floor. He'd begged me to calm down. He'd even tried to stroke my head before one of the other scummers pulled him away into the TV room with the others.

As the afternoon dragged into the evening, all I could see was his face, creased with worry as he bent over me. And all I could think was, *Why was he telling me to calm down? Why wasn't he climbing on Ronnie's back, telling him to get off me? Backing me up?*

And the more I thought about it, the guiltier I felt. By the time I'd got the twins to bed (with no mention of the restraint from either of them), my head was fit for bursting, so I'd taken myself down the fire escape and fifteen minutes later found myself staring at the light in their hall, a rock in my hand.

As soon as I'd seen the light I knew I had to get in there. It was too good an opportunity to let slide. I knew, God knows why, that peace lay inside. Well, relief at the very least.

I breathed deeply and stared at my watch.

Quarter past ten.

Perfect timing, but as I lifted my eyes to the house, I knew instantly I was out of luck. The hall light was on, perfect, but so was the landing light. And the light was on in their bedroom as well.

They were in, and it looked like a regular night in the Scott house. I could see them in my head, Jan faffing about in the bathroom, while Grant would be dreaming about one more can of lager, knowing he couldn't get away with it without having his ear bent.

They were so easy to read. So predictable. That was until the front door opened and Grant appeared, leaving me to dive back into the shadows.

He scanned the street a few times, frowning, checking and rechecking the time on his watch.

I was thrown by the break in routine and didn't know whether to stay where I was or make for home. After all, there was no way I was getting my head down in there tonight.

By the time I looked back at the house, Jan had joined Grant on the doorstep, stroking his arm gently before leading him back inside.

Leaving me pretty much out of options.

Freeze my arse off outside or head back to the scummers, hoping they hadn't checked my room yet.

The streets in our town are like wind tunnels.

The road that leads to school is dead straight and at least 200 metres long.

Cycling up it is always murder. The wind just batters you.

Gets into every crease of your clothing and underneath your bike until you honestly think you might be going backwards.

I used to battle it, though, see it as a challenge.

Push through it by telling myself it would be easier on the way home when it was beating at my back, helping me along.

Except it never did.

It was always exactly the same going home. The same endless hurricane gusting into your face, wobbling you with every push of the pedal. I swear I used to look across the road to the cyclists going in the opposite direction, wanting to shout to them. Ask them if they understood how it was possible. What we could do to make it all just that bit easier.

But I tell you what. I never got off the bike. Not once.

I wasn't going to let it beat me.

And I wasn't going to let it beat me tonight either.

So, as I felt the first gusts rip at my coat, I lifted my collar to my chin and looked it in the eye – completely unaware that I was walking into a storm that I'd never come across before.

One that might just get the better of me.

CHAPTER 7

I clocked her pretty early. As soon as the allotments came into view.

She was wrapping her coat as far around herself as she could, burying her chin into her chest, hiding her face from the wind.

Maybe that's why she never saw them.

I'd seen them already.

It was rare for the bench by the allotments to be empty, even on the coldest nights, and there were three of them huddled there, passing a can quickly between themselves. I didn't recognize them, mind, not the usual crew. They were older, which confused me, because if I'd been them I'd have been in the boozer rather than freezing my nuts off for a four-pack of Bulmers.

It didn't seem to bother them, and from the crap they were spouting as I approached on the other side of the road, I knew they'd downed a few already. Enough to fend off the cold at least.

As I drew level with them, I kept my head up and eyes fixed forward, not wanting to show any weakness they could pick at, and for whatever reason it worked. They continued to ramble some nonsense and I ghosted by.

I knew it wouldn't be the same for her. No matter where she looked.

In fact, I'd only gone a few seconds past them when they caught whiff of her.

'Oi, oi, eyes right, fellas. Eyes right.'

'I've got you. Tidy, mate, very tidy,' followed by drunken snorts of laughter.

I heard a can spin into the road as they stood, the echo splitting the silence.

Not that it was quiet in my head. The blood was still pounding in my ears as I fought off the frustration of not getting into Jan and Grant's. The prospect of another sleepless night in my room wasn't helping either. If it had been warmer I'd have plonked myself somewhere with a can of something as well. Drowning myself in cider had worked enough times before.

But I wouldn't drink with those lads. I'm not squeaky clean, granted, but there was something about them that reeked. As I walked on, I hoped the girl could smell it as well.

I glanced at her from across the street as we drew level. Her face, what I could see of it, was blank.

Emotionless.

Fixed forward.

Which meant she must have seen them.

I looked again at her eyes.

Did I know her?

I felt like I did but I couldn't quite place her.

I slowed, not breaking step, just putting the brakes on a bit.

She'll cross in a minute, I thought, quicken her pace, and if she's got any sense she'll whip her phone out and make a quick call. Let whoever is expecting her know that she's only seconds away, even if she isn't.

I winced.

Why was I giving this a second's thought?

What did it have to do with me anyway?

If she was dumb enough to find herself in a situation, then fair dos. Deal with it.

But as I reached the corner that led back towards the dual carriageway, my feet slowed and I found myself looking back.

That niggling sense that I knew her stopped me, and instead I hugged the shadows and peered back towards the allotments.

Their jeering was building, but her pace wasn't. She just marched on, oblivious.

'Where you off to, then, petal?'

As if they cared.

'Aye, there's no rush. Come and have a drink with us.'

As she drew level with them they fanned themselves across the pavement, leaving her no option but to cross the road. Or plough straight through them.

Which is exactly what she did.

With no fuss.

Without raising her hands, she just marched through them.

It took them by surprise of course, especially as the meat-head holding the can was left wearing the cider rather than necking it.

'You dozy cow,' he yelled. 'Look at what you've done.'

The fact that his two mates were wetting themselves didn't do anything for his mood and so he scuttled after her, waving his finger pointlessly at the back of her head.

'Oi!' he screamed. 'Oi! Where do you think you're going?'

His voice rose in anger with every step she took. And when she didn't break stride, two things happened that I didn't expect.

One.

Instead of pulling her round to face him, or running ahead of her, he simply grabbed her by the hair, yanking her head back so hard I expected a load of hair to come off in his hand.

Two.

Instead of crying out in pain, like anyone else, the girl spun on her right heel and delivered a right hook to the guy's cheek, so hard, so clean, that I heard the impact from thirty metres away.

His hand, still gripping her hair, whipped to his cheek as he crumpled to the floor, and he curled into a ball, as if expecting a flurry of blows to rain down.

With that, it all kicked off.

The laughter stopped and was replaced by a manic roar, as the other two lads charged at her.

Maybe she knew she had no chance of outrunning them, but whatever the reason, she wasn't bricking it enough to leg it. She just looked at them as they sprinted towards her. In fact, her gaze didn't drop until the first dickhead backhanded her straight across the cheek, knocking her to her knees.

All thought of walking away gone, I ran at them.

Even with one of them on the floor, the chances of me gaining an advantage were pretty small. After all, they weren't kids. They were handy. This wasn't new to them by any stretch.

So I needed any element of surprise possible.

This worked well with number one, who went down quickly after a meaty forearm to the back of his head. But before I knew it, the other lad was on me, sticking my head into a lock before bending me in half and ramming his knee to my cheek.

The floor spun as it reached up to greet me, but no sooner had it met my head than I was back on my feet, arms pinned behind my back, as the guy I'd whacked staggered towards me, picking the grit from his palms.

'This just gets better and better. You this dozy cow's fella, are you?' he gasped with delight. 'What's the problem with the two of you? No manners, either of you.'

He unloaded a left hand into my belly, before straightening me up with a knee to the forehead.

My head was buzzing, ears ringing. But I wasn't done. There was no way, after the day I'd had, that these losers were going to leave me in the gutter.

He ambled closer, smiling to the meathead still pinning me from behind. But he milked it for too long, allowed me enough time to refocus on him, and as he reached striking distance I swung my leg flush between his, catching him square in the bollocks.

He stumbled back, grabbing his balls as if they were in danger of rolling away, so I turned my attention to the guy holding me from behind. As he peered over my shoulder in the direction of his mate, I flicked my head backwards, catching him on the nose. Not hard enough to put him down, but enough to make him lose his grip.

I turned, the adrenalin starting to pulse through me as I shoved him backwards.

'You've got a nerve talking about manners,' I yelled. 'Three meatheads like you going after some bird. What sort of perverts are you?'

Without hesitation I put him on the floor. And kept him there, with one kick.

Then another.

Another.

Another.

The top was off the bottle and there was no way I was stopping.

Until I was on the deck again, lumped from behind.

As I rolled over, hands wrapped around my head, I could see the first guy, the guy who went for the girl, leaning in on me, his face twisted in anger, his cidery breath even angrier.

'Who do you think you are, eh? You think you're Superman or something? Truth is, sunshine, you should have left well alone. This had nothing, NOTHING, to do with you. But it has now. You've made something out of nothing.'

I saw something flash at his side and knew it was a blade. Didn't need to see it. Just knew, instantly, that he was going to cut me up without a second's thought.

I lay there.

Still.

But I didn't take my eyes off him. There was no way I was letting him know I was scared.

Because I wasn't.

No one had pulled a knife on me before, but I'd been in far darker places and I'd always got back on my feet.

I felt madly invincible, untouchable. As if I *was* some kind of Superman.

I started to laugh. Which threw him, and made him madder. He paused, as if to check what he was seeing, and as he bent over me, something flashed behind him. Not a knife, though, something blunter and heavier. And with that he fell on top of me, blocking my view of the starry sky above.

CHAPTER 8

It took so much effort to heave the body off me that I wondered if I'd see a lump of brain stuck to the spade in her hand.

Not that it bothered her. She stood over his body and chucked the tool on top of him, before turning to me.

'He's not going to wake up for a while, but I don't fancy being here when he does.'

She scooped up her bag from the floor and turned away.

'Hang on a minute,' I yelled as I got to my feet. 'You all right?'

'Me?' she said, without turning back. 'Nowt wrong with me. I'm not the one who took the pasting.'

'But that lad properly caught you one back there.'

She still didn't stop, but did spare me a glance, an angry mark hugging her face.

'I'm fine. I only got caught with one. You're bleeding, you know.'

I wiped at my nose, a streak of blood on the back of my hand.

'It's nothing. He caught me flush, that's all.'

'Oh, right. Good.'

And that, it seemed, was that.

She flicked her bag back up on to her shoulder and strode off, as if I didn't even exist.

It took me a second to realize that, as far as she was concerned, it was game over.

I shook my head quickly, as if the whack had altered my take on what had just happened.

If I hadn't waded in, she would've been in deep shit.

I'm not really one for manners, but I reckoned she owed me a 'Cheers' at least. So I took off after her, jogging to keep up.

'And that's it, is it?' I said, to the back of her head.

But the back of her head wasn't up for talking.

So I said it again. But the silence went on.

'I said, aren't you forgetting something?' and without thinking I grabbed at her shoulder.

Big mistake. She swung on her heel, just as she had minutes before.

As her arm whipped around, I craned my neck backwards, out of instinct rather than judgement, and felt the wind brush my chin as her fist flashed by.

'Jesus,' I cried, 'what's the matter with you? Don't you realize what just happened back there? Those lads were going to kick your arse!'

That seemed to grab her attention.

'What? Until you jumped in, you mean? Am I meant to be grateful or something? From what I remember, the arse taking the biggest kicking wasn't mine!'

As she spat the words at me, she looked me in the eye for the first time, and again I was left with the nagging feeling that I knew her. But I still didn't know why.

I was sure I'd remember someone as narky as her.

'Hang on a sec. The only reason I took a kicking was you. I was on my way home. I only stopped because that lad left half of his hand welded to your cheek.'

'So what do you want, then?'

'Want? I don't want anything. Look. Forget it. I hope you get home OK.' And with a last glance in her direction I shook my head and turned away.

'Wait,' I heard, at least I thought I did, but not loud enough to make me stop.

'I said WAIT.'

Loud enough. So I turned back.

She hadn't moved. The same blank look, the same glazed eyes. The only thing changing was the size of the bruise on her cheek.

'Look,' she said. 'I'm grateful. I am. I'm just not big on saying it. And I didn't ask you for help either, remember.'

'Fair dos.'

'So let's just call it quits, then, shall we? You helped me. I helped you. End of story.'

And then she did something unexpected. She raised her hand, waiting for me to shake it.

I didn't take it straight away. I just stared at it, making sure it wasn't a crappy joke. But grudgingly I stepped forward, extending my own hand in turn.

Her fingers were cold, but so were mine. And as we shook hands, I could feel her iciness thaw a bit. At least I thought I did. Her face hadn't changed, she just looked me straight in the eye, but I could tell she was checking me out the same way I had looked at her.

I'd swear she was looking at me, wondering if she knew me too.

The moment swept past as she dropped her hand and turned away.

'Hang on a minute,' I shouted after her. 'Have you got far to go?'

'Why? What are you going to do? Walk me home and keep me safe?' A smile flickered across her face.

'Just wondering, that's all.' There was no way I was going to offer unless she asked.

'I'm staying round the corner, with mates.' Although she didn't look too chuffed about it. 'I'm sure I won't need you between here and there.'

'I'll see you, then.'

'Yeah, maybe.' And she walked on, hands thrust in pockets.

As she walked away I realized that in the minutes since the guy had lamped her, she hadn't once winced or raised her hand to her face. Hadn't once even acknowledged that she had a bruise the size of a tennis ball growing on her cheek.

It was then that I realized I *hadn't* met her before. But I did know her all the same. I was sure of it. I'd put money on it. If I had any.

Because she was like me.

She was a lifer too.

CHAPTER 9

Ronnie's words rang in my ears as I pushed through the classroom door.

'Keep your head down today, Billy, will you? Just try and, you know, blend in.'

I sighed at the chances of trying to go unnoticed, especially at school.

It had never been an option before.

By the time I started infants properly, stumbling as I counted from one to ten, the other kids were practically on to their times tables.

It was pretty obvious I wouldn't ever be on *Countdown*, let's put it that way. And when you're struggling, it's hard to go unnoticed. Most of the time there'd be an extra member of staff with me, explaining stuff again and again, trying to get it straight in my head how it all worked.

Of course it didn't take long for the other kids to pick up on it, and even when kids are seven years old, they still know how to wind you up. Still know how to pick a fight with the different kid in the class.

And it wasn't only the kids who knew I was different. It was just as bad with their parents.

I'd see them, stood in their little groups at the gates, wondering who'd be dropping poor little Billy off that day. I'd see them shaking their head as they clocked the fifth different scummer collecting me that week. Obviously, they never felt sorry enough to invite me round to tea, to come and play with their kids. Eat off their plates, run around in their garden. It wasn't sympathy they had for me. It was pity. And it was easier for them and their kids to try and pretend I wasn't there than try and get to know me.

By the time I hit eight or nine, it was worse. The gap between me and them was getting bigger by the day, and I knew it. And of course I didn't like it.

But they did. They loved it.

And by now little Billy, the class idiot, was becoming Billy Finn, career lifer. The older kids back at the home had toughened me up, leaving me ready to pass it on to anyone daring to take the mick. I wasn't fussy about where I dished it out. Schoolyard, footie pitch, classroom, it was all the same to me. As long as people got what was coming to them, I was happy.

Teachers didn't quite see it that way, though. They didn't agree with my kind of 'education' and insisted that one of the scummers was with me at all times. Can you imagine the embarrassment?

It was like shoving a sign on my desk that yelled KID IN CARE. KID IN CARE.

Ronnie, naturally, revelled in it. Made a real point of getting to know all the other kids' names, and when they asked if he was my dad, he'd just chuckle softly and say, 'No. Not his dad. Just his uncle. Uncle Ron.'

As far as the other kids were concerned, I came from the biggest family they ever saw. They'd meet a different auntie or uncle pretty much every day.

At least today I was walking into the classroom on my own, without Ron hovering in the shadows, pretending to be something he's not, or could ever be. Let's face it, he's never had to restrain one of his own kids in the middle of a classroom, has he?

Arriving on my own still had an effect, though, because as I stomped through the door, the room fell silent. No one in my class, it seemed, had been warned I was on my way back.

'All right, Billy?' risked a voice from the back, obviously crapping themselves already.

Everyone else just dropped their heads or pretended to carry on with what they'd been doing.

I glanced round the room, looking for the best place to sit, knowing I had to put a marker down. Make it clear that although I hadn't been in for a few months, I was still someone to keep well clear of. Unless I told you otherwise.

I made for the back of the room, stopping by Danny Shearer's desk.

Danny was one of those annoying kids who seemed to be brilliant at whatever he fancied. You know the type. Sport, acting, school councils. He popped up everywhere and, for some reason, the other kids still seemed to like him. Respect him even. The perfect person to make my point with.

'You're in my seat.'

Twenty-nine pairs of eyes fixed on Danny, who was bricking it too much to even look up.

I gave him a few seconds, but he kept his eyes on his desk.

'I said, you're in my seat.' And I cuffed him round the ear. Not a full-strength back-of-the-hand, but enough to send a pleasing slap around the room, and enough to cause an intake of breath from everyone in it.

I saw the anger flare in his eyes and my own breathing quickened as the prospect of a face-off sprang to life.

'What was that for?' His face was suddenly millimetres from mine.

'It's pretty simple, Danny. You weren't listening, were you? And from what I remember, you're not a soft lad. So if I were you, I'd park my arse somewhere else sharpish.'

I could see the thought process flick across his eyes as he stared into mine. He had a choice. He knew he was a big lad, knew that if he really fancied it he could have a go at mixing it up with me. And he knew that if he did start something, there were a dozen other lads who would stand up with him if needs be.

On the other hand, he knew who I was, and that even if him and his mates got the upper hand now, there was always later.

It only took him a second to grab his bag and scuttle to the other side of the room. His next-door neighbour took the sensible option of quickly following him, leaving me the luxury of a double desk to myself.

I can't say it felt good to have scored the early point, but it was definitely a relief. I knew that if I was to get through the next few months, and prove to the Colonel and the others that the twins were best left with me, I had to deal with the whole school thing. And the only way that was going to happen was if the other kids left me alone. Hence the early marker. If they thought I was crazy enough to pick a fight in my first minute back, then maybe they'd keep away full stop.

Of course, school or no school, my plans were really in trouble if what I overheard from Ronnie was true. I had to find a way of getting into Annie's head, find out if she really was after taking the twins home. And if she was, I had to find a way of stopping her.

I opened my school book and scrawled 'Annie' at the top of the blank page. It seemed as good a time as any to start formulating a plan.

By the time Thursday arrived, my ideas to derail Annie had come to a shuddering halt.

Aside from taking the twins and running, robbing banks along the way, I'd come up with exactly . . . well, nothing. Which was disappointing, given the amount of time I'd had to come up with better.

Singling out Danny Shearer certainly had the desired effect, though. The rest of the kids had given me a seriously wide berth. As we walked into class each morning, I could see them nervously standing about, almost fearful of sitting down in case I told them to move. Perfect. Meant I didn't have to do it again, not for a while at least.

The surprising thing was that the teachers showed no interest either.

Not even the friendly 'welcome-back chat' with the Head that I normally got. Well, I say friendly; it was usually the first of several final warnings before the inevitable suspension.

'So, Billy, tell me, what is going to be different this time around?'

'Sir?'

'Come on. What has changed in that brilliant mind of yours to make me think that we won't be meeting on a daily basis?'

'Don't know, sir. Probably nothing, sir.'

'Tell me something, Billy, will you? What exactly are you hoping to get out of school?'

'Same as everyone else, I suppose. Learn and stuff. Get a decent job.'

'And what would that job be?'

'Dunno.' I'd shrug. 'Something that pays enough to sort out the rent and buy the twins whatever they need.'

Whenever I said this, he'd shake his head and ramp up the lecture.

'You know, you have to start applying yourself, Billy. This mythical job you think you're going to walk into when you leave here? Well, let me be frank. It doesn't exist. Not without application here and now!'

'Yes, sir. I know, sir.'

'No, I don't think you do. You aren't the first child in your position to walk in here. I've taught so many others like you, you know.'

'Not sure I understand, sir.' Although I did. I just wanted him to feel awkward when he had to spell it out.

'You know. Young people who are without . . . who don't live with . . . who are in the care of the local authority.'

Could he make me sound any more like a statistic?

'I've worked with children who have experienced the

same things you have. Lived in the same places you have. But the difference between them and you is that they viewed school as an opportunity. As their chance to make sure they didn't make the same mistakes as their parents. Do you understand?'

'Yes, sir.'

'Good man. I'd like you to know, Billy, that the staff here want nothing more than for you to succeed. To leave here with everything you need to get that job, that house, those nice things for your siblings. We are here for you, Billy, so use us. Those other children did and they've gone on to good things.'

After that he'd excuse me, with a final warning that he didn't expect to see me again before the end of term.

Funny, I could have sworn he'd just told me his door was always open . . .

And all that crap about other lifers making good? Well, it was news to me.

The other lifers I knew had careers all right, but not the sort you bragged about. Last time I heard, sweeping roads or working in the prison kitchens wasn't the job of legend the Head made it out to be.

I didn't know whether to be relieved or upset that he'd ignored me this time around, but I was surprised when most of the other teaching scum took the same approach. Aside from my ageing form teacher, Mr Barnes (who taught German and insisted on weekly one-to-ones), the others gave me a wide berth.

Old man Turner in French didn't even bother collecting my exercise book at the end of each lesson. He was spot on of course, as he'd find shag all written inside, but still, it was his *job*, wasn't it? I thought for a second about telling the Head, the sheer lunacy of the idea of that conversation bringing a rare smile to my face.

So, as the first week dragged into the second, which in turn fizzled into the third, I could feel the routine of school slowly rotting my brain into obedience. I was here, and I was keeping my head down, but it wasn't doing me or the twins any good.

All that changed, however, on the third Tuesday morning.

I was slumped as usual, ignoring my name being hollered by Barnes as he tried to complete the register, when the door opened and the Head walked in, with what looked like a new kid in tow.

I didn't really pay much attention to be honest. I knew I'd done nothing to hit his radar and I certainly wasn't interested in babysitting some newbie for the next few days. Not that they'd ask me. That'd be like putting a drunk in charge of a boozer.

'Good morning, everyone,' he chimed. 'Apologies for the interruption, Mr Barnes, but I wanted to introduce you all to a new member of your class. This is Daisy Houghton. Daisy has just moved into the area, so I expect you all to set her the finest example and welcome her to our school.'

And then he turned to leave. Not that I bothered looking up.

Not until Barnes piped up anyway.

'Welcome to our happy band, Miss Houghton. As you can see, we are rather stretched for space, so for now I'd suggest you take a seat next to Billy Finn there. Second to back row.'

There was a splutter of giggles, but not from me. The last thing I needed was some new bird expecting me to show her the ropes, so I flashed a look in the direction of the gigglers, before yanking my bag from the desk beside me.

'Billy?' boomed Barnes, clearly revelling in my unhappiness, 'I expect you to be a gentleman towards our new class member. No biting, do you hear me?'

The braver members of the room let a laugh bounce around the walls and begrudgingly I lifted my eyes to my new neighbour. I had to give her a look that told her not to bother getting friendly, that this arrangement wouldn't be for long.

Unfortunately, that look didn't quite reach her. As I lifted my gaze to hers for the first time, I was confronted by a sight that I didn't expect.

It was her. The girl from the allotments. The girl from the fight.

And in that split second, I knew that my plans for school were in bits.

That from that moment on, there would be no chance of an all-new, low-profile Billy Finn.

CHAPTER 10

If she was surprised to see me, she certainly didn't let it show. In fact, she barely spared me a glance as she slipped into the chair next to me.

Straight away I recognized the expression she had worn throughout our meeting by the allotments. The same icy glare, the same ability to stare with force without focusing on anything at all. I didn't have a clue what she was thinking about, and just like the last time, it was annoying and impossible to ignore.

There I was, two weeks into the world's longest school silence and all of a sudden I had this ridiculous urge to talk to her. About what, or why, I had no idea.

I wanted to check her out, see if the bruise on her cheek had gone, but there was no way I was going to sit there and give her the satisfaction of starting things going.

So I did the unthinkable and opened my textbook. The words didn't make sense, but to be honest they didn't before she arrived. I had three and a half minutes to kill until the bell for end of registration. Hardly a difficulty, given the endless periods I had dozed through since returning, but with every passing second I felt more uneasy. I just hoped she wasn't picking up on it. From the silence ringing on her side of the desk, it didn't appear to be bothering her none.

As the bell rang, I leapt to my feet in relief, knocking the chair to the ground as I sped for the door. I don't think Barnes knew what was going on. I was usually in no hurry to get to first lesson. In fact, he usually had to evict me, threatening to walk me to my next class unless I got 'my arse in gear'.

I hadn't a clue where my next lesson was, or what it was for that matter. I just wanted to try and understand why the arrival of Daisy Houghton was playing with my head.

I spent the first period in a spot I'd made my own since coming back, the store at the back of the school gym. It was rammed full of crap: rusted old hurdles, sacks of deflated footballs and, most importantly, crash mats. The type they use for the high jump and pole vault in the summer. Big and saggy, like the best beanbag you ever flopped into. All right, they didn't smell too clever, but neither did most of the kids in my class, and no one commented on them, did they?

Jan and Grant had had one of those beanbags. You know the ones. As big as a settee, they were, and when you fell into them they just moulded and clung to you. Most comfortable thing I ever sat on. Almost made me feel guilty, it did. I could never believe I'd fallen on my feet so well as to find a family who had such a thing. I certainly never deserved it.

Lying on that mat made me relax, I guess. Took me back to Jan and Grant's. Allowed me to think about stuff. About this girl who was freaking me out.

She just made me feel uncomfortable. I'd had this school

thing all sorted, knew exactly what I had to do and how, but with her there, even for those few seconds, I could feel it slipping away. Like she had the measure of me, even though she'd barely looked me in the eye.

Well, bollocks to that. I couldn't let anyone get to me. Especially some ungrateful Doris like her. So what if she was here? I'd done her a favour the other week after all. Without me the rozzers would have been scraping her off that road for days. She probably realized that now, I thought, as I heaved myself off the mat.

Once we'd broken the ice, she'd probably fess up and be grateful. It'd be fine. Just as long as she didn't expect any gratitude back from me.

Avoiding her wouldn't have been too difficult if it wasn't for registration. It was these two periods of the day that threw us together, and thanks to me terrorizing Danny Shearer, she had no option but to park herself next to me every time.

The silence we'd set up since she arrived was the same every day. In fact, we built up a kind of awkward routine which involved her slumping next to me, while I inspected the muck on my shoes until the bell rang. This was my excuse for a swift exit, more often than not for the refuge of the gym, leaving her to stare into space, or whatever oblivion she was focusing on.

This carried on for a good week, and no matter how much I tried to persuade myself otherwise, it was getting to me. I had to fight the temptation to speak to her, to go over what had happened that night. To check she was OK and, most importantly, to try and confirm my hunch about her being a lifer.

As it turned out, I didn't have to wait much longer, as Daisy broke the deadlock before I burst it.

I was sat in the corner of the schoolyard, fretting about Annie and the twins, when a voice interrupted me.

'You got a light?'

The sun burned my eyes as I lifted my head. It took me a second or two to work out who was even asking, and another moment to believe it was actually her.

I patted my chest and trouser pockets far too eagerly, even though I knew there was no light in there. After all, I didn't even really smoke.

'Er, should have. Just can't put my . . .'

'Well, either you do or you don't. Which one is it?'

'Must have left it at home,' I mumbled, adding 'sorry' before I could stop myself.

'Don't worry about it. It's hardly worth smoking anyway. I've been rolling them thinner to make the baccy go further, but I can hardly taste it. Waste of time.'

I nodded in agreement as I tried to regain some sort of composure.

'So, how's it going, then?' I risked. 'You been back to see the Head yet?'

'What makes you think he's interested in me?' she said, as she rifled through her bag.

'I dunno. Just making conversation, that's all.'

For a moment there was silence, with only the rustling of paper as she searched her bag, swearing to herself as she did it.

'Got you!' she shouted, a smile licking across her face for the first time as she lifted a battered Zippo to the fag in her lips.

She inhaled deeply, before blowing the smoke into the air, breathing new words at the same time.

'Five times,' she said, letting her gaze fall back to me.

'What?'

'The Head. He's had me back in there five times. Wants to save me, he does. Knows how to do it as well, apparently.'

She swung the bag over her shoulder and headed for the gate.

I smiled with recognition, as my own conversations with the Head merged with hers.

I knew it. I knew it.

'Oi!' came her shout, breaking my train of thought. 'You coming, then, or what?'

I fought the temptation to look around. This wasn't the time to cement her opinion of me as public dickhead number one.

'Your choice, Billy Finn. You can stay and let the Head offer you salvation, if you want, or you can come with me.'

'Where are you off to?'

'God knows. But it can't be worse than here, can it?'

That was good enough for me, and I allowed myself a smile as I followed her out of the gate.

CHAPTER 11

It felt good to be out of school. After all, there hadn't been a whole lot of learning going on for the past three weeks. Unless you counted learning how to jump through the Colonel's hoops.

The freedom seemed to be rubbing off on Daisy too.

'So where've you been hiding?' she asked.

'What do you mean?'

'Well, you've not been in many classes. You seem to disappear after registration every day.'

I didn't have a clue how to respond to that. I had no idea that she'd even noticed me, so I reacted in the only way I knew how. Aggressively.

'Who are you, my mother? I didn't realize the Head was paying you to look out for me.'

'Easy, tiger,' she said with a smile. 'Just trying to make conversation.'

'Well, maybe you should've tried that the other week, right after those lads were kicking your arse.'

She looked surprised, amused even.

'Are you still cut up about that? I thought we dealt with that on the night.'

'Yeah, well, I don't particularly enjoy getting knives pulled on me.' I thrust my hands into my pockets. 'Funnily enough, it's not how I choose to spend my evenings.'

'Good job I was there, then, wasn't it?' She laughed and then paused, before adding, 'You don't have to thank me, by the way.'

Talk about being difficult. She was impossible to score a point against, so I let it drop.

'Did it take your cheek long to heal?'

'Nah.'

'What did your friends say when they saw it?'

'What friends?' she mumbled, head falling to the ground.

'The friends you're staying with. They live near the allotments, don't they?'

I was digging for information and she knew it.

'Oh . . . them. They didn't say anything.' But the way she pushed her hair nervously behind her ear told me otherwise.

'Hell of a bruise, though. Must have been some size the next day.'

'Nothing a bit of ice and some make-up couldn't fix.'

I thought back to the bump she'd worn that night. It was no small bruise. It was threatening to take over her face after a few minutes, so it would have been a full-on shiner by the next morning.

'What about you? What did your folks say about your nose?'

'Ah, you know . . .' I shrugged, wiping at my nose instinctively, almost expecting it to be still bleeding. 'It's not the first time, let's put it that way.'

'Really?' she said, with a smile that lit up her face. 'You

76

surprise me. I heard you were a proper choirboy. I can't imagine you ever getting in above your head.'

I let that comment hang there for a minute or two, unsure of what to say. Wondering who had been talking to her and what they'd said.

Although she was finally talking, she wasn't giving anything away. Nothing that made me change my mind about her. Something about her told me she had to be a lifer. I just couldn't work out what it was.

It wasn't the way she looked. I mean, she was pretty normal. Bit on the skinny side, but so were loads of the lasses in our year. And she didn't go for the whole fake-tan thing either. At least I didn't think she did. I'm no expert.

She *was* decent-looking, I suppose. But maybe that was because she didn't seem to care. She was always wearing jeans, and shirts that were too big for her. She had this habit of hanging on to her sleeves, which were too long for her arms. She was constantly gripping the cuffs between her fingers and the palm of her hand, which made her seem smaller than she actually was. She may only have been five foot three or something, but she was impossible to ignore.

I was trying not to stare, but it was difficult. In fact, it wasn't until she caught me looking that I realized how I knew for certain about her.

It was her eyes. The way she looked at things. There were times she'd stare at something for what seemed like minutes at a stretch, but there were times, like now, when her eyes flitted from left to right, then up and down, as if she was endlessly looking for something. Something important.

I do that all the time, especially when I think I'm going

to lose the plot. It feels like if I'm not taking everything in as it happens, I'm going to miss something. Something I need to chill out. Something I can't live without.

I can't tell you what that something is, there are so many things missing. So many things that give me the fear. Like losing the twins, or growing up to become like Annie or Shaun.

But I knew, *I knew* for sure, in that instant, that she felt the same. So I went right for it.

'I wanted to walk on that night, you know.'

It took her a minute to latch on to my train of thought, and when she didn't jump in, I just continued.

'The night with those lads. I wanted to walk on. Ignore what was happening, but I couldn't. Because as I passed you, I had this weird feeling that I knew you. You know what I mean?'

She looked none the wiser, but she was definitely listening.

'It's not like me, you see. To stop like that. It's not what I do. I'm not into the whole Good Samaritan thing.'

'Look,' she interrupted, 'I told you before, I don't do thank-yous. Can we not just leave it?'

'It's not about that. I'm trying to explain. Trying to make sense of why I did it. And why it is that ever since, every time I see you, you give me the fear.'

'What do you mean "the fear"? What have I done –'

'Just listen, will you? I'm trying to say something to you, tell you something. The reason I stopped that night is cos I thought I knew you. But I didn't, I know that now. But I also know – at least I think I know – that we're the same, me and you. I'm sure of it. We've seen the same things, haven't we, in different houses like, but the same things anyway?'

As the words fell out of my mouth, it was like someone else was saying them. They sounded desperate, mad. They were the truth, the words I'd wanted to get out since that first night, but outside my mouth they sounded ridiculous.

To me anyway.

All Daisy said was, 'Fancy going halves on a bag of chips?'

The chips tasted great. Daisy had gone mad with the salt and vinegar, but they gave us something to fill the awkward gaps in conversation, and gave me something to drown my embarrassment in.

'Sorry about what I said back there,' I muttered, shovelling another chip into my mouth. 'Don't know what came over me. I just have these mental ideas sometimes and I don't know what to do with them.'

She hadn't said anything about my outburst. Nothing. Which made me think that I must have got it wrong. But as she dragged her last chip across the salty paper, she finally piped up.

'Nothing to say sorry about. I know it's not easy.'

'What do you mean?' I was confused.

'I heard things. From the kids at school. Well, I mean I overheard them.'

I didn't like the sound of that. 'Oh aye, what sort of things?'

'That you were in care. Had been for a long time, and that you had a brother and sister.'

'Oh, right.'

79

'Look. I don't want to make a big thing about it. In fact, I don't want to talk about it at all. But I understand. I do. I know what it's like. To not live with your folks and that.'

My head pounded at those words, at the fact that I'd been right all along. But there was such sadness in her voice that I felt guilty for forcing her into a corner about it.

'I didn't mean for you to have to talk about it. Forget I mentioned it. They're not even worth talking about, parents. I wish mine were dead.'

Daisy sniffed as she chucked the chip paper into the bin.

'That's the problem, Billy. Mine already are.'

Rummaging in her pocket, she pulled out a pile of change, counted it and sighed.

'You got any more cash?' she asked. 'I fancy getting wrecked.'

CHAPTER 12

The Friday night freak show was never something to look forward to. Not in my book anyway. Being dragged out and stared at by normal people wasn't my idea of fun, but it was a ritual we were forced to endure every week.

The scummers always reckoned that a 'house' night out was good for us. Showed us what it meant to be part of a family. Have you ever heard such a load of cack?

How many families do you know that have ten kids and four carers in it?

Or how many families turn up at the cinema in a minibus?

The staring would start as soon as we arrived. We were never the smartest-looking mob, or the quietest, and you'd see parents guiding their kids away as soon as they clocked us. I swear that some kids were once hoicked out of the swimming pool as soon as we dipped our toes in the water. That's how contagious we were.

Some weeks, when I really couldn't face the embarrassment, I'd kick off on a Friday afternoon, just to give them the excuse of grounding me. All right, it was boring at home on your own, but at least it was quiet.

The only problem with that plan was the twins. When I

was banned from going, they got upset, and if they missed out as a result, then the Colonel started giving me grief, telling me I was spoiling it for them.

So more often than not I went along, desperately hoping that I wouldn't catch sight of anyone I knew.

Where we went depended on who was on shift. The brighter scummers chose the cinema, for two obvious reasons. First, it was an enclosed space, making it harder for us to do a runner, and second, it meant they got through nearly two hours of their shift without having to speak to any of us.

The newer bods, though . . . well, they made some terrible decisions. Like taking us to Laser Quest. I mean, I'm not the sharpest tool in the box, but even I know that putting guns in the hands of ten angry kids is never going to be a good idea. Not for us, or for the spoilt kids that found themselves terrorized as we ran rampage.

The worst night happened just after me and Daisy had started hanging out together. We weren't together all the time or anything, but a few nights after school we'd trawled round town, looking for anywhere that would sell us some booze.

One Friday night she'd suggested doing something, and looked put out when I told her I had to join the regular lifers' freak show.

'I can't think of anything worse. Can't you get out of it? There's a band playing in town and I reckon we could get in easy enough.'

I'd mulled it over, but the thought of the twins' disappointed faces was too much to bear. For a second I'd worried that she was going to ask if she could join us instead, but after a shrug and a mumbled 'never mind', she'd let it drop.

We'd ended up going bowling that night. And on the way the rest of the lifers were pretty calm. Little wonder with Ronnie running the show.

The only problem was, he had a couple of temps with him, and although this happened a lot, none of us had ever seen these two jokers before.

They were classic temp staff. Smiley, eager to please and utterly useless.

As soon as I saw them climb into the van, I knew the evening was doomed.

They spent the journey trying to make themselves popular, cracking lame gags to the younger kids, who giggled along because they didn't know better.

Once we got to the bowling alley, though, they were completely out of their depth.

What normally happens is this:

Ronnie parks van.

Ronnie turns round and reads the riot act about good behaviour.

Ronnie gets lifers to sign contract in their own blood, promising good behaviour.

Ronnie singles out Billy for extra promise on good behaviour.

Doors are then, and only then, unlocked, leaving lifers to walk like zombies into the bowling alley.

But unfortunately, as soon as the van was parked, one of the temps made the fatal error of opening the door, and we all sprinted inside before Ron could suck the life out of us.

From there it all went downhill.

Instead of having ten kids to look after and organize, Ronnie had ten kids and two scummers to sort out, and from what I could see, we were less of a problem than they were.

It took them twenty minutes to get us out of the arcades and another fifteen to get us into the right bowling shoes. Ronnie tried to act as shepherd, guiding the temporary scummers like dogs, but he would have had more joy had he just waded in and picked us up by the ears.

Eventually, we were plonked on to two lanes, much to the dismay of a group of lads in their late teens next to us, who even at first glimpse were taking their bowling far too seriously.

You know the type. They'd stand for thirty seconds, drying their hands before even daring to pick the ball up. Then there was the ridiculous posing as they lifted the ball to nose level, as if whispering to it, telling it how many pins to knock down.

Naturally, I took great delight in laughing when all they managed was to whack over a measly couple, drawing disapproving glances every time I snorted.

When they did manage a strike, you should have seen the celebrations. You'd have thought they'd won the World Cup or something, not successfully tossed a ball down an alley. Each one had their own little dance, shuffle or lame moonwalk, and it wasn't long until we were all imitating them, whether we'd knocked over any pins or not.

They tried to ignore us, and Ronnie did his best to calm us down, but he couldn't handle all ten of us on his own.

Things really kicked off, though, when Charlie Windass

dared to pick up one of their balls. I don't know if he realized it was theirs, but he wasn't the type to care anyway.

What he did know is that, for some reason, he was winding them up, and he loved it.

Lifting the ball to his nose, he danced to the edge of the lane, not realizing one of the fellas was running after him.

As he swung the ball backwards, he managed to catch the guy full in the stomach, like something out of a slapstick movie. With that the other guys on the lane rushed forward, yelling at him to put the ball down.

Of course Charlie did the exact opposite, running halfway down the lane, until he was only a matter of metres from the pins. But instead of rolling the ball into them, he hurled it, like he was playing cricket. The sound as the ball obliterated the pins was deafening and I swear, in that second, the whole alley stopped in its tracks.

Full of himself, Charlie moonwalked back down the lane, arms aloft, straight into the owner of the ball, who gave him a mighty shove for his trouble.

Something flicked in Charlie's head. I'd seen him kicking off at home, witnessed it up close and personal, and knew that once he went into one, it could take him an age to calm down.

He launched himself at the guy, who was nearly six foot and twice his weight. More out of surprise than anything, the guy fell on to his back, leaving Charlie to throw himself on top, arms flailing.

I've never seen Ronnie move so fast, but I'm not sure he knew where to go, towards Charlie or into the path of the other fellas, dashing to their friend's defence.

In the end he settled for Charlie, dragging him away, putting himself between Charlie and the angry group.

He then threw his arms in the air in submission and tried to explain what was going on.

'Lads, lads. I'm sorry. Listen to me, will you? Let me explain. He didn't understand . . .'

But with his arms waving wildly, Ronnie had let go of Charlie, who took the opportunity to dart around him and deliver another series of kicks and punches in their direction.

Finally, the temps got themselves into gear and wrapped themselves around Charlie, dragging him away to safety.

The rest of us didn't know what to make of it. The younger kids thought it was just about the most exciting thing they'd ever seen and were egging Charlie on. All I did was keep a guiding arm round each of the twins, making sure they were out of reach of any loose punches that were being thrown.

As the scummers sat on Charlie, Ronnie went into a full charm offensive, whipping his ID out of his pocket like a rozzer.

I hated it when he played the ID card. It was one of those things that the other lifers probably never noticed, but I'd seen it time and time again. Whenever things got a bit fruity, whenever he found himself in an embarrassing situation, he always played it.

It made him out to be some kind of saint for looking after us wild kids and I saw the guys checking it out, listening while he gave them the sob story about us. Within a minute, their body language had changed, pity replacing their anger.

Charlie, however, was nowhere near calming down. The temps had never seen anger like it, or a crowd the size of the one that was now surrounding them. It was a car crash and the people watching were loving it.

'What are you looking at?' Charlie screamed, his arms crossed in front of him like in a straitjacket. 'Why the fuck are you looking at me?' His face was straining as he tried to shake his way out of the temps' grasp, and with every effort, you could see his temper spiralling out of control.

And that's when it happened. Something I'd never seen before, or want to see again. Desperate to shake himself free, Charlie sank his teeth into one of the temps' hands, snarling like a dog as he did it. The temp recoiled in shock and shook his hand free, but somehow he managed to hold Charlie in the same straitjacketed position.

'Don't you bite me!' he spat. 'I'm trying to help you here. You wouldn't bite yourself, would you, so don't bite me.'

Charlie was so out of control, so in the zone, I was surprised that he heard what was said to him. But not as surprised as when he did what he was told and bit into his own arm.

Why he did it I don't know. Maybe it was the crowd staring, maybe it was the fact that he didn't really know the two scummers pinning him down. Maybe he was just afraid, but once he'd bit down on himself, he wasn't prepared to let go.

All of a sudden, the crowd weren't quite so happy to watch. Kids were quickly led away, while a few others turned their backs in shock. Some filed out once Ronnie piled into the scene, telling them to back off.

All I could see was Charlie's face, twisted in anger as his jaw locked upon his own arm.

Being restrained is the worst thing in the world. Worse than being cuffed by a rozzer. At least then you can move your arms a bit and your legs are free. When you're being pinned down by two bruisers, nothing moves, no matter how hard you try.

There've been occasions when I've pretended to calm down, only to lash out once they've let go, but I've never been tempted to hurt *myself* like Charlie did.

I pulled the twins into me, blocking their view, and watched as Ronnie tried to take control. But at first his presence only seemed to make things worse.

He bent down beside Charlie, stroking his head and whispering calmly into his ear.

But whatever he said, it wasn't enough – although it was for one of the temps, as tears started to fall down his face.

It's not often you see the scum cry. All right, you might see some crocodile tears when one of the lifers moves on, but not like this. This guy was out of his depth and he knew it. He couldn't even wipe the tears away for fear of Charlie landing a right hand on him.

At that point, Ronnie stepped up a gear, swapping places with the tearful scummer, before lifting Charlie to his feet. As the angle of his body changed, Charlie had no option but to open his mouth and let go, and as he did all I could see were deep tooth marks in his arm and broken, bloodied skin.

Flustered and embarrassed, Ronnie marched towards the exit, whispering to a still-angry Charlie.

I looked round at the rest of the lifers, and saw nothing but shock and tears. All they wanted was to be back in the van, home and safe. But there was no way our temp friend was going to get us there. Which left me with no choice.

'Right, then,' I barked. 'Get your stuff together. And quickly, if you know what's good for you.'

Naturally, we were back in the van in minutes, quiet and shocked, hoping Ronnie and Charlie wouldn't be far behind us.

CHAPTER 13

Days at school didn't pass any quicker with Daisy around, but they were more bearable, I suppose. Maybe it was reassuring to know that someone else found it as useless as me. Maybe it was to do with not being the only lifer there. I don't know. Can't say I really analysed it.

To be honest, despite Daisy's weird choice in clothes, I was still the stand-out loser in our year. She had this annoying habit of blending in. She didn't walk down corridors, she ghosted down them. When she entered the room, I swear sometimes the door didn't open before she came through it. She was anonymous, and that was the way she liked it.

That didn't mean she was an airhead, though. She took everything in. She was a real people-watcher and, man, was she brutal at picking them apart.

I started looking forward to breaks in lessons. In the past, I'd skulk around the yard, looking for someone to start something with, but now, with Daisy in tow, we'd plonk ourselves in the middle of them all and laugh our tits off at how shallow they were.

For the girls, it was all boys, clothes and, for the wilder ones among them, the clubs they were getting into that weekend. As for the lads, it was football or talent. Nothing more. In their words, 'What else is there?'

It was alien to me. The way they spoke, the families they talked about. I couldn't imagine them having to plot ways of keeping their brother and sister away from their alcoholic mother. But I wasn't jealous or envious. I just didn't know any different.

Sometimes I'd watch Daisy's reactions to it all. She'd sit and stare, her mouth snaking into a smile as some dizzy bird mouthed off about the new dress Mummy was going to buy her that weekend. She'd stare so hard, it was as if she was trying to take in every second, storing them all up in her head like an endless stream of photos.

'Why do you find people so interesting?'

She shrugged, although she knew the answer off by heart.

'Suppose it's a bit like watching a film.'

'That's your thing, is it? Films and that?'

'Absolutely,' she said, her eyes sparking for a second. 'I'd be in the cinema every day if I could. Doesn't matter what's on, I'll watch it.'

'I've never got it really. I don't want to go and watch a comedy, cos most of the time I haven't got a clue what they're all howling at. And it just reminds me how little laughing there is at home. And as for action stuff, well, they're a right load of old bollocks. They're not realistic at all, are they? It never makes *that* noise when I smack someone in the face.'

'Use your imagination, Bill. It's good to escape inside something else for a couple of hours.'

'You're kidding?' I smiled. 'By the time it had finished,

someone would have been in my room and nicked every-thing.'

She pushed me away with a grin and told me she'd show me the light if I wanted, but before I could answer the bell rang and we slumped our way to the next lesson.

We didn't have every class together, due to the fact that she was smarter than me. It wasn't that she kissed up in class or worked dead hard or anything either. She just seemed to know what she had to do to make people leave her alone.

It suited the teachers perfectly. The quiet kid among thirty gobby ones was hardly going to get picked on, were they? As I said before, she wanted to ghost through school, and she was succeeding.

Or rather she was until she was late for one of Carrick's classes. Carrick ran his classroom like Ronnie ran the house. For years I thought they must be related, or have been grown in the same test tube or something. They were anal beyond belief and loved to inflict as much pain on their kids as possible.

Carrick was the only teacher who had his own classroom. All the other teaching scum moved around the school to teach the different years, but not him. His room sat next to the Deputy Head's office and was the only one in the school that was locked between lessons.

When you had geography with him you had to line up along the wall outside and wait for the door to be unlocked, then he'd announce, 'Good afternoon, everyone. Please take your seats. I'm sure I don't have to remind you that your desks are numbered and are, as always, spotlessly clean. Sit yourselves in your usual position and leave the classroom in the same state in which you find it.'

The room was always tidy. Freakily so. There was never anything in the bin, any posters on the wall and certainly no chewing gum stuck under the desks. Carrick caught a kid trying once and had him in detention for ages, until he'd scraped the gum off every desk in the school. I think the kid was about twenty-five when he finally finished.

At the start of each term, he allocated you a desk, with the class sat strictly in alphabetical order. This meant I'd struck gold, as I got landed next to Daisy, and we sat halfway back in the class, our desks and chairs numbered identically.

He seemed to take an instant dislike to Daisy, probably because she arrived mid-term, meaning he had to rearrange his seating plan. He couldn't possibly sit someone whose surname began with an 'H' next to Pete Tanner. That would mess his head up completely.

Whether Daisy picked up on his dislike, I don't know. She just turned up and went through the motions as usual, until the day she came in fifteen minutes late.

I'd been wondering where she'd got to. She'd been there to register in the morning, but then we'd sloped off to different classes. When she didn't show I just presumed she'd gone to the dentist or something, and cursed my luck as I wondered who I could blag the answers off for the rest of the lesson.

When she arrived she looked more like she'd been on the operating table than in the dentist's chair. Her face was completely white and her steps were small and uncertain, like she was having to concentrate on every move she made.

She didn't look in Carrick's direction as she picked her

way to our desk and he waited until she reached her chair before piping up.

'Good afternoon, Miss Houghton. Thank you for joining us. Would you kindly come out to the front of the class please?'

I could see her flinch at his words. This was her idea of hell. Thirty pairs of eyes fixed on her, all of them grateful not to be on the end of whatever was coming next.

Slowly she traced her way back to the front of the class and faced him, her back to the rest of us.

'Turn round please.'

'Sorry?' she whispered, her voice only just reaching me.

'I said, turn round and face the class please.'

She wheeled round, her head falling as soon as it came into view, her hair masking what bit of her face we could see.

Carrick leaned back in his chair, his hands clasped behind his head.

'Perhaps you'd like to explain to the rest of the class why you have arrived late. After all, twenty-nine of them, thirty including me, managed to arrive punctually.'

His words hung in the air as Daisy's head remained pointed at the floor.

'Well?' he asked. 'There must be a reason. You can't now, after – what? – six weeks here, have suddenly forgotten where to go. And as the rest of the class will have to remain with you after this class ends, to make up the time you've missed, I think the least you could do is explain it to them.'

A twenty-eight-strong groan rang around the walls and I could feel my face burning up. She was the centre of attention, the focus of the whole room, and I didn't have a clue how she was going to react.

And what did she do?

She did nothing. She just stood there and didn't move. Seconds became minutes and I could feel the heat in the room begin to rise with the tension of it all. Daggers were being drawn and all of them were pointed straight at Daisy.

Carrick seemed hell-bent on humiliating her to the max and leapt to his feet, before pacing up and down behind her, lingering over her shoulder as he spoke.

'That's three minutes, Miss Houghton. Added on to your initial fifteen minutes, of course. Are you ready to explain yourself now?'

When nothing passed her lips, I could see the first wave of irritation waft over him and he stepped it up a gear.

'If you're so loath to give us a reason, then perhaps you can tell us why the rules should be different for you?' He fixed her with a stare and, just for a second, I saw his eyes flick up and down at what she was wearing. 'Are you any different from the rest of the class?'

Nobody bothered stifling their sniggers, despite the evil glances I was throwing in their direction. Now Carrick was in full flow, they were more than happy to join his pack, and he lapped it up greedily.

My blood was threatening to boil over, when I caught a glance from Daisy. It was brief and masked by the hair hanging over her face, but I could see it was telling me to cool it. That me strangling him wasn't going to help. So, much as I didn't want to, I followed her plea.

I reckon a good five minutes passed before Carrick finally

sent her to her chair, telling everyone they would stay behind for twenty minutes once the bell had rung.

'Let this be a warning to you all. I will not tolerate tardiness. When you arrive in this classroom it is always prepared for work. I expect nothing less from you. The day you arrive in this room and it is not ready for you, the lesson will be over, and frankly you can all go home!'

Sermon over, he fell back into his chair and returned to his marking.

Detention over, the rest of the class sped out of the room, the majority of them flicking evil glances or snide comments in Daisy's direction.

The chair clattered down behind me as I leapt from my seat, and had old man Carrick not jumped down my throat, someone would have been in deep trouble.

'Whatever it is you're about to do, Mr Finn, take it outside this room and outside the gates. I will not tolerate fighting.'

With a little help from Daisy, we left in peace and saw the other kids beat a hasty exit for the streets around school. I was in no rush, though. There was something I needed to do before heading home.

'You all right, mate?' I asked Daisy, her face still empty of colour.

She nodded slowly. 'Just feeling a bit crappy, that's all.'

'No need for him to lay into you, was there? He's such a control freak.'

We walked slowly towards the gate and, as we passed the teachers' car park, I felt the devil rise in me.

'Listen. Keep your eyes peeled, will you? I'll only be a sec.'

Crouching low, I ducked between the first row of cars. I always made a note of which car belonged to which teacher. Why? For moments like this, when a little bit of payback was in order. It didn't take me long to find Carrick's car. It was the cleanest in the school obviously, but by no means the newest, and my eyes skipped over it to see what I could get stuck into. The aerial was the first thing and it bent easily. I took care not to snap it off completely, using just enough force to leave it knackered. I wondered if I had time to let a couple of the tyres down, but with teachers as desperate to leave as the other kids, I settled for a long scratch down the driver's wing. I smiled as I scampered back towards Daisy, picking the yellow paint out from the grooves in my key.

My hero bit didn't seem to improve her mood, though, and to be honest it didn't really set the score straight either. He'd gone out to humiliate her in front of the whole class and nobody would see the state of his car except him. No, this was going to need some thought, and with the end of term only a couple of days away, I knew I had to do some fast thinking.

As it turned out, the school holiday played right into my hands, although I had my work cut out to get things sorted in time. But when Daisy and I left school on the Friday afternoon, I had a smile and a half on my face. And it had nothing to do with a break from the place.

By the time we lined up outside Carrick's room at nine thirty on the first Monday back, there was already a sense of confusion in the corridor. Everyone was stood, single file as always, but asking the same question: 'What is that smell?'

Carrick was definitely asking it as he breezed down the corridor, but it wasn't enough to stop him launching into his usual speech.

'Good morning, everyone. I trust you all had a restful break and are ready to apply yourselves. You all know where your seats are, so take them quickly please and apply yourselves to your work.'

With that, he jammed his key into the lock, but he stopped as his nostrils flared and he turned to face us.

'What is that smell? If the offending article is in one of your bags, make sure it does not come through the classroom door. Am I understood?'

As he turned his attentions to the door handle, I couldn't resist whispering to Daisy, 'Listen. Things are about to kick off. Just follow my lead, all right?'

'What?' she mouthed, but it was too late as we filed in, Carrick counting heads as we moved past him.

By the time half the class were inside, the queue stopped moving and the smell was suddenly overpoweringly minging.

I could see the panic on Carrick's face as he scoured the queue, trying to work out just who was responsible for it.

'Come on, come on,' he yelled. 'Can you please get yourselves inside? You can't have forgotten where you are meant to be sitting already.'

But when nobody moved, he lost his rag and pushed his way into the room. And that's went things got really interesting, because instead of the neatly arranged rows of numbered desks and chairs, there was just this pyramid mess of wood and metal in the middle of the room. Every desk, every chair, except for two, had been pushed into the middle of the room and they'd all been stacked randomly on top of each other. I had to admit it looked even more impressive than I remembered. There was no order to it, no symmetry or reasoning behind what went where. It was just this big sprawling mess of legs and numbers.

The rest of the class had spread out around it, mouths flapping open. There would have been more laughter had the smell in the room not been so appalling. Kids were glancing around the room, noses upturned, as they tried to fathom out just what it was and where it was coming from.

I wish I could have snapped Carrick's face as he clocked his precious room. At first he looked shocked at the mess, but no sooner had he seen it than the smell really invaded his nostrils. His head flicked from side to side as his focus zoomed from smell to desks and back again, and I could practically hear his stress levels rise as his ordered little world crashed around him.

Daisy beamed from ear to ear at the carnage.

'Genius, Billy Finn, genius,' she whispered in my ear. 'When you said things were going to kick off, I didn't expect this.'

'I'm a man of hidden depths, me.' I laughed. 'What did you think I'd done? Just spat on the door handle or something?'

'Probably, yeah.'

'Well, I did that as well, obviously.' It wasn't easy stifling the laughter swelling in my chest. 'But I thought we owed him a bit more than that. Look. Follow me.'

Walking slowly around our classmates, who were still giggling and retching in equal measure, I led her to the two desks and chairs that sat in their usual places. Desks and chairs that just happened to be ours.

Sitting quietly, we unzipped our bags and took out our exercise books and pens, arranging them neatly on the desk.

'Tell me that smell is your handiwork as well, will you?' she muttered.

'Yup,' I answered. 'See that ventilation grille on the wall by his desk? There's been half a dozen mackerel fillets rotting in there since –' I glanced at my watch theatrically – 'ooh, since the last Friday of term.'

I thought she was going to fall off her chair when she heard that. 'You're kidding me? How did you even get in here? Carrick guards it like Fort Knox.'

'Managed to nick the keys from the secretary's office on the last day of term, didn't I? Spun her some sob story about needing extra lunch vouchers, and while her back was turned, bingo.'

'I love it,' she said, giggling. 'Did moving all the tables and chairs take long?'

'Not really. I waited till everyone had gone for the day and the cleaners had done their bit. Didn't matter if I made a racket then.'

We sat back like a couple of angels and watched the chaos brewing around us.

Carrick didn't know what to do with himself. At first he thought he could sort it out and started pulling at various table legs. But when that started an avalanche, he thought better of it and bellowed at the rest of the class to move to the edges of the room.

I pitied the poor kid who ended up stood next to the air vent by Carrick's desk, but his reaction was priceless.

'Bloody hell, sir,' he wailed. 'Smells like something's died in your drawer or something.'

Carrick dashed to his desk. He looked in danger of losing the contents of his stomach by the time he got there, and certainly seemed relieved when he opened his drawers to find them empty.

By now his face was reddened and sweaty, and he was out of ideas, until his eyes met us, sat bolt upright at our desks, textbooks open in front of us.

'Houghton, Finn,' he boomed. 'I want a word with you outside now!'

I rose slowly from my desk and started packing my stuff into my bag.

'I'm sorry, sir, but as the room obviously isn't ready for us, I can only presume that this lesson is over for today. Shall we leave you to tidy up? I can't imagine your next class will be too happy to work here either.'

I swung my bag over my shoulder and paused at the edge of my desk, waving Daisy before me. With slow steps we paced towards the door, feeling the delight grow as the rest of the class fell into line behind us. We marched noisily down the corridor, past the Deputy Head's office and through the doors to the yard.

I couldn't resist taking a peek through the window as we passed Carrick's shambolic classroom. I don't know who had taken it worse, him or the Deputy Head, who seemed to be tearing a strip off him for losing an entire class.

It always felt good to get one over on the scummers, whether it was at home or at school. And as we headed towards the gates, we knew this one was going to be talked about for months to come.

CHAPTER 14

The giggling from behind the bedroom door kind of gave the surprise away.

Not that I was still asleep. Birthday or otherwise, I'd seen the sun come up as normal. But for the sake of the twins, I forced my eyes shut as they edged closer to my bed.

I heard a clatter as something landed on the bedside table, followed by a whoosh of air as they launched themselves on top of me.

'Happy birthday, Bill!' yelled Lizzie as she landed on my back, although Louie seemed more interested in my present, or at least in opening it himself.

I allowed myself a smile as I pulled the pair of them close to me. Birthdays as a lifer were never days to remember and definitely not days to look forward to. Not when you'd endured as many with Ronnie as I had. Getting cards from the twins was fine, but there was always a card missing. The one you really wanted. The one that never came.

'Look, Bill, look!' yelled Louie, as he rammed a handful of envelopes under my nose. 'Look how many you've got! Open this one first, our one.'

I flicked through the small handful of cards, knowing

instinctively who they were from without even opening them. Louie and Lizzie, the other lifers (not that they'd thought of it themselves), the scummers, Ronnie (why he bothered, I never could work out), Dawn (our social worker for that month) and, finally, a neatly written card that went quickly under my pillow for later.

'Thanks, you two, that's brilliant,' I said, forcing a smile as I saw the 'world's best brother' greeting on the front. It tore me apart to think that it could be the last time they'd be with me on my birthday.

'Open your prezzie, Bill. Go on, open it. Open it!' gushed Louie, dizzy with excitement.

'Why, what is it?' I laughed, knowing full well what was inside the small silver packet. The same thing as every year. The same thing Louie always chose.

As I slid off the wrapping, I grinned the grin he wanted to see.

'Footie stickers!' I cried, watching his face light up in turn. 'Brilliant, you two. Thanks!'

That was Louie's cue to snatch them from my hand, ripping the stickers from the packet as he shuffled them through his fingers, agile as a poker player.

'Whoooa. You've got Gerrard. And Crouch – that's really rare, that is!'

'Is it? But I've got them two already. So why don't you do me some swaps and keep them yourself?' I lied. It was present enough to see him beaming.

'BRILLIANT! Cheers, Bill!' he hollered, before launching himself from the bed and scampering off to his room, tearing the back off the first sticker as he ran.

Lizzie just stared at me.

'Sorry about the stickers, Bill,' she said, frowning. 'I wanted to get you something different this year, but Louie was practically crying in the shop.'

'Don't be daft.' I grinned as I pulled her close again. 'I love them, you know I do.'

Over her shoulder by the headboard was a mural of footballers' mugshots. My trophies from celebrating too many birthdays as a professional lifer.

Real presents were never a good idea. Not for lifers. Christmas especially.

To be fair to them, the scummers always try to put on a good show, always make sure all the kids have got a decent number of prezzies. And by the time all ten kids have opened everything, it's like being trapped inside the Argos catalogue. You can't move for trains and dolls and bikes. It never lasts, though. All that good feeling. All the ho-ho-ho. Especially when you can see the carers checking out their watches, counting down the minutes to the end of their shift, so they can get home, give out the proper presents, be with their real kids.

Ronnie would practically sprint out of the door at the end of his shift. Could never wait to get home and shower his *real* boys with prezzies.

The lifers pick up on it. Course we do. We don't want to be there any more than they do. So by the time the new shift comes on at five p.m. Christmas Day, all they get is a sink full of pots, a floor full of broken toys and the prospect of half a dozen restraint reports to write by dawn.

Happy fucking Christmas.

Nah, a packet of footie stickers and a hug from the twins are good enough for me.

'Right then,' I groaned, as I pulled myself from the bed, only to be stopped by Lizzie.

'Where are you going, Bill?' She looked worried, eyes as wide as saucers.

'Breakfast, chuck. If I don't get down there soon the Colonel will have locked the cupboards till lunch.'

'But you don't need to. It's Saturday and we brought you breakfast in bed.'

And there it was, on the bedside table. The biggest plate of breakfast I'd ever seen. Cereal, boiled egg, juice and the fattest, greasiest bacon sarnie I'd ever clapped eyes on.

'Look at that!' I yelled, as the prospect of another breakfast scuffle magically disappeared. 'That is without doubt the best present you've ever given me.'

I folded her into my chest. I'd have left her there forever as well if I thought the bacon would keep warm somehow.

'He said you'd like it.' Lizzie beamed. 'Said he'd put money on it.'

'Who?' I mumbled through a gobful of bread. 'Louie?'

'No, not Louie.' She laughed. 'Ronnie. It was his idea.'

The words stuck in my throat as I practised them in my head. Lord knows how it would sound if I actually tried to thank him for my breakfast.

I mean.

What was it with him?

He could've made the twins feel like it was their idea.

Why did he have to take the glory?

It was only a bacon sandwich after all. If he thought he could make up for all the years of lies with one breakfast, then he was dreaming.

Anyway, he probably only did it to avoid a scrap at the breakfast table. Last thing he wanted before going home was to have to pin me to the table. Wouldn't be the first time he'd written up a birthday restraint.

By the time I'd got dressed, I was ready to blow. In fact, he'd given me the perfect excuse to have a pop at him about keeping secrets about the twins and Annie. Breakfast in bed couldn't excuse that and he knew it.

I'd reached the bedroom door before I remembered the card still under my pillow. As hard as I tried to shake it from my head, I knew there was no way I could go down the stairs without opening it first.

It wasn't a big card. Just a plain white envelope with 'Mr B. Finn' written carefully on the front. I turned it over in my hands, second-guessing what was inside. Would it be the same as last year? Or was it something new? Maybe they'd changed their mind after all and realized they'd made a horrible mistake. As the thoughts raced through my head, I ripped at the envelope, yanked the card open and scanned the lines written inside:

Dear Billy,
We hope this card finds you well and that you are
enjoying your fifteenth birthday. It seems hard to believe
that another year has passed so quickly, doesn't it?

Not to me, I sneered, wondering when she was going to get to the point.

> *Grant and I wanted to send our love to you, and let you know that although we haven't seen you for so long, you are still in our thoughts.*
>
> *We hope that both you and the twins are well, and that you are getting on well with Ronnie. He's great at dropping us a line occasionally to let us know your news – we do love to hear how things are.*
>
> *We had no idea what to get you this year, but thought this voucher would allow you to choose something yourself.*
>
> *Thinking of you on your special day,*
> *Jan and Grant*

Ripping out the ten-quid voucher, I scoured every centimetre of the card for a message from Grant, before realizing that he had only signed his name next to Jan's. No message, no small talk, just his name, signed no doubt at his wife's insistence. Three years may have been a long time for Jan, but obviously not long enough for him.

Throwing the card across the room, I couldn't believe I'd allowed myself to daydream. Why on earth would they change their mind now? They'd made their decision. I wasn't what they were looking for. Wasn't what their dream had been.

Pushing the resentment to the pit of my stomach, I headed for the stairs. There was no way Ronnie was getting his thank-you now.

Luckily for him, our paths didn't cross that morning. In

fact, after the first hour had passed, I just presumed he'd gone home.

Typical. He couldn't even be arsed to wait around on my birthday. Some 'uncle' he was. He probably had something planned with his boys. Football or out for lunch. Whatever it was you did with your own kids.

As lunchtime ticked nearer, my mood deteriorated. It may have been my 'special day', but that didn't alter the fact that it was Saturday, and that meant losing the twins to Annie for the afternoon.

The prospect of seeing her swanning off with them was just too much to bear, so I pulled the phone from my jacket pocket and hit Daisy's number. No sooner had her answerphone kicked in than I felt someone tap me on the back. I killed the call, cursing my luck, before spinning to face the Colonel, who, despite sweating, was all smiles.

'Blimey, Bill. You could try cracking your face. It won't fall in half just cos you manage a smile.'

He was lucky I didn't lamp him there and then. In fact, had he not jumped in straight away, I think I probably would have done.

'Come walk with me, big lad. There's things that need to be said.'

Of course this got my back up instantly.

'What makes you think I want to listen to you? Think breakfast in bed makes us mates, do you?'

Ronnie just creased his face in surprise. 'What? Oh, do give up, Billy. That was just for starters. We need to chat, me and you. And when we're done, then your birthday can start properly.'

'What's that supposed to mean?' I yelled as he marched away.

'You'll see, sunshine, you'll see. Come on, fall in!'

There was no answer to that. Apart from wandering after him, giving him the finger as we walked.

CHAPTER 15

Fortunately, the march only lasted for a minute or two. Just long enough to get us across the field towards the old garages. Ronnie didn't stop frowning the whole way, which usually meant trouble of one kind or another.

Just before we reached the knackered old buildings, he pointed towards a bench.

'Perch yourself on there a minute, Billy. There's something we need to talk about.'

'You're all right. I'd rather stand.'

If he thought I was going to make anything easy for him, he could think again.

I saw his shoulders sag a bit, as the first part of whatever he'd planned started to unravel.

'It's about Annie,' he said. 'Well, kind of. About her and the twins really.'

I felt the tension start to rise in my gut, as the words I'd dreaded edged closer.

'As you know, Annie's been seeing the twins regularly now for a good while. Eighteen months it's been, without a contact session missed. And Dawn and me, well, the whole care team, we've seen a big change in her. A sustained change. I'm guessing you've seen it too.'

I stared at him as he let the question hang there. What was he expecting me to do? Agree with him?

'Well, it's been decided that it's in the best interests of the twins if this arrangement is developed. Accelerated, if you like.'

You couldn't make it up, could you? The crap he was spouting. *Accelerated*? He was talking about my family, not watching *Top Gear*.

'The care team have decided that contact between the twins and Annie will be increased to three times a week, and that she will be allowed unsupervised contact on Saturdays.'

It was getting harder to keep quiet as the anger crept to my fists. But as hard as this was for me, I wanted it to be harder still for him. I wanted to hear him struggle as his lies came tumbling down around him.

'I can't even begin to think how difficult this must be for you, Bill. I know what the twins mean to you. And I've seen – we've all seen – the efforts you've made since your review. But we have to think about the twins in this. They're nine years old, mate. And they've been here eight years. It's too long! You know it as well as I do. But this could be *their* chance. Annie's chance too.'

'Her chance?' I spat. 'Don't you think she's had her chance? She had her chance ten years ago and she didn't take it. She chose Shaun, didn't she?' I felt sick at the mention of his name. 'She chose him and she chose booze. She didn't have to, but she did. That was her choice. *That was her chance.*'

Ronnie rubbed at his forehead with one hand, deflecting my pointed finger away with the other.

'People change, Bill.'

He tried to hold on to my arm, long enough that for a second I saw only Shaun.

'They do change, mate. Do you not think that Annie regrets what she did? She has to wake up every day knowing that her three kids are in care.'

'Two kids,' I blurted. 'She has two kids. She's not my mother. I'm not her son.'

'She'll always be your mum, Bill.'

'She hasn't been my mum since she signed those papers, Ronnie. Since she told Jan and Grant they were welcome to me.'

'Oh, Billy, she signed those papers because she thought it was best for you. Three years ago she was in a different place. She probably never thought she'd get to where she is today.'

'And where does that leave me, then?' I yelled, before realizing I'd said too much. I stared at the ground, trying to pull the anger back from my fists, trying to swallow it down as I had done so many times before.

'Come on, then, Ronnie,' I growled. 'Give me the big truth. How long till you take them away from me? How long till you let her loose on them all over again?'

'Let's not get carried away, Bill. We're not setting any hard and fast timelines to this. Annie doesn't want us to either. For the past six months she's been going through a period of evaluation. She's been seen by doctors, by counsellors, by social workers, and they've all been analysing where she's at; how she might cope with the twins coming home. If she copes with the extended contact, and if the twins respond too, then we'll look at overnight stays, then weekend visits. Returning home full-time could still be a year away.'

'But it could be sooner as well, couldn't it?'

He couldn't even look me in the eye as he nodded.

'I'm not going to lie to you, Bill. It could be less, yes.'

I shook my head in disbelief, my balance split between launching myself at him and just turning and running. I couldn't work out which would be best. And I wasn't even sure if I cared.

'How long have you known about this?' I had to know if he had the balls to tell me the truth. 'How long have you been planning it all behind my back?'

'It's not a conspiracy, Billy. This has been discussed for a long time, probably about a year.' He must have seen the pain in my eyes as he said it, as he took a step towards me, arms outstretched. 'And we talked so often about when to tell you, when might be the right time.'

I shook my head in disbelief. 'And that's now, is it? On my birthday? Outstanding, Ronnie. Out. Standing. In fact, tell you what, why don't you let them go swanning off this afternoon with Annie as well? Oh, yeah,' I added with a snarl. 'You already are!'

He looked like he'd been stabbed. Like he was the one hurting.

'There was never a good time, Bill, was there? I've wanted to talk to you for weeks about it, but you seemed to be doing so well. Like you were turning a corner. So I hung on. I was wrong, mate, I realize that now.'

'That's big of you.'

'I know this must be a shock, Bill. I know it must feel like the end of the world. But it's still early days and a lot can change, believe me.'

The problem was, I didn't believe anything was going to change. Nothing ever did around here.

'Kids belong with a family. I believe that. I have to. It's why I do this job. So please try and believe me, we're doing this for all the right reasons. The twins need a family.'

But not me, I thought, as the last glimpse of fire went out.

'Look. I've got something for you. Something I've been working on for a while now. And I think you'll really like it. Think it might help, even.'

I couldn't believe my ears. All of a sudden it was my birthday again. Forget the fact that he'd just told me he was tearing me and the twins apart, now it was time for jelly and ice cream.

'I want nothing from you. Do you get me? Nothing. So go home, Ronnie, or piss off to your boys, or do whatever it is you do when you finish your shift. Just don't give me anything. I don't want it and I don't want you.'

Conversation over, I skulked back to the house, although the gate seemed like a better idea. As much as I wanted to bolt through it, I knew it wasn't an option. Annie was due in two hours and if there was a chance, the smallest of chances, that she wouldn't show, I had to be there. For the twins. After all, it wasn't their fault. Just everyone else's. Mine included.

CHAPTER 16

The key jumped in my hand as it scraped along the length of the car, but it was an empty feeling. Didn't give me a buzz or shift the clouds for even a second.

Whichever way I looked at it, whatever I chose to trash, the truth remained the same. I was losing them. In fact, I'd lost them already, lost everything.

Annie had turned up of course. Bang on time and full of herself.

Lizzie had been waiting impatiently, her face glued to the porch window, counting down to the moment she could race through the door and into Annie's chest. A full-force hurricane of a hug, the type usually reserved for me.

I didn't hang around once she arrived. Louie stood next to me, as he always did, but I knew he wanted to be out there, doing the same as Lizzie. So after telling him to have a wicked time, I sloped up the stairs and into my bedroom.

Not that I was sticking around. After folding all my cards (except for the one from the twins) into my back pocket and grabbing my jacket, I was off down the fire escape, tapping out a text as I went.

Luckily, it didn't take long for the phone to buzz, and luckier still, it came with the answer I'd hoped for:

```
C U at the alltmnts in 10
```

Stupid really, to think that the bench by the allotments had become our meeting point, but it had never crossed our minds to stay away. The lads that had gone after us that night hadn't ever turned up again and we hadn't given it any more thought. It was just our spot, the place we ended up on the way back from school, or during it for that matter.

In the few weeks since we'd stitched up old man Carrick, we'd ducked out of lessons a fair bit, but we tried to be clever about it. The teachers never complained even though they must have noticed we weren't there. They were probably just chuffed to have the hassle that came with us removed from their classes.

We didn't always leave the grounds either. I'd introduced her to the gym store room and we'd chill out in there. Sometimes talking. Sometimes not.

It wasn't like we were up to anything in there either. I liked her and that, cos it made a change to feel chilled out around someone else. Not to have to worry about what they made of me, or that they were only there out of pity.

When I spoke, it was pretty much about nothing. It wasn't as if I was up to speed on world events or anything. All I knew was life at home and the Colonel, and God knows how bored she was listening to me bang on about it.

Daisy, on the other hand, seemed to know a load about everything. Music, books, cinema especially. She told me about films that sounded so amazing, and in so much detail that I felt like I'd already watched them. In fact, I'd sometimes close my eyes as she talked and let pictures take over in my head. Of course I only did that when she was on the other side of the room and couldn't see me. Didn't want her thinking I was some kind of loon.

The only thing she didn't talk about was herself. Since that day with the chips, any mention of her being a lifer had been off limits, and while she was happy to listen to me moan about the Colonel, she never mentioned the friends she was living with or, more importantly, what had happened to her folks.

And I was cool with that. I still wondered of course, but what point was there in pushing?

Sat on the bench, knees bouncing as the adrenalin buzzed around my body, I started to wonder if Daisy was going to pitch up. The last thing I needed was a no-show. Fifteen minutes later, I'd pretty much given up, and had started wishing that Jan and Grant had sent me cash instead of a voucher. What I needed was a bottle of something, not the chance to buy a new pen.

Just as I was ready to go, she appeared. And for the first time since we met, she looked flustered. She practically flew around the corner and I could see her muttering to herself, arms waving dramatically.

Throwing herself down beside me on the bench, she reached for the tobacco in her bag and set about busying her hands. It wasn't until the cigarette was rolled, lit and in her mouth that she managed to get a word out.

'So what's up with you, then?'

'Same as you by the look of things,' I offered, trying a smile. 'Other people being a pain in the arse.'

She laughed through her nose, a cloud of smoke billowing out of her nostrils. But it was only a moment of humour before the frowns returned to both of our faces.

'What kept you?' I asked. 'That was the longest ten minutes I've ever known.'

'Don't even ask. They decided we'd be spending the day together. Problem was they didn't bother to ask me first. What is it with adults? Do they honestly think we get a buzz out of spending time with them?'

I leaned forward, my interest pricked by the mention of the 'friends' she was living with. It was the first time she'd offered even the tiniest glimpse of her home life and I was trying to find a way of looking interested without seeming desperate to know more.

'Do they do it a lot?' I asked.

'What?' She'd resorted to her usual trick of zoning out.

'Your friends. Do they always want to spend time with you?'

'Not if I can help it.' Flicking her head towards me, she was back in the conversation. 'So what's going on with your lot? The Colonel on your case again?'

'Nah,' I mumbled, wondering whether I even wanted to mention it. 'It's just that today's meant to be my birthday and that.'

'So what's your problem? You should be celebrating. Going out with the twins or something.'

She was right, and the truth of them being with Annie more than pricked a bit.

'Yeah, that's part of the problem.' And before I knew it, I was giving her the full low-down on the day. The twin's breakfast, Ronnie's part in it and the run-in we had afterwards. I even went as far as spilling all the details about Annie's plans, and although it felt good as the words came out, it just cemented my depression by the time I'd finished.

'So this is all I have to show for my birthday,' I said, pulling the cards from my back pocket.

'At least you *got* some cards,' Daisy offered, as she relit her fag.

'I'd rather have none than any of these. I mean, look at who they're from. A bunch of kids who can't stand the sight of me, a bunch of adults who only care cos they're paid to, Ronnie – well, enough said on him – and this one,' I barked, pulling Jan and Grant's to the top of the pile.

'Who's that from, then?'

I paused for a second before going on. 'Aw, just this couple. I went to stay with them a few years ago, but it – well, it never really worked out.'

'Why? What happened?'

'Dunno,' I lied. 'Just never liked them really. They were a bit weird. Had all these funny ideas about how it should be in their house. And when I disagreed, they didn't like it. I sacked it off in the end, got my social worker to send me back to the twins.' It almost sounded believable as the lies fell out of my mouth.

'So why did they send you a card, then?'

'Dunno. They're weird is all.'

She reached forward and took the card from my hand.

'Let's see what they said, then. They sound bizarre.'

But that didn't feel right. It was OK for me to slag them off, but not anyone else. Besides, the last thing I wanted was her seeing what was written inside.

'Oi. Don't snatch that off me. It's private, that is.'

'Chill out, Billy, will you?' she muttered, thrusting the card back into my hands. 'I thought you said they were a bit weird. I just fancied a laugh, that's all.'

'Yeah, well, have a laugh at someone else.' I was sick of being the butt of everyone's crappy gags. 'Here, pass me your lighter, will you?'

She reluctantly passed it over after sparking up her rollie again. She spent more time lighting her fag than actually smoking it. Hardly seemed worth the effort.

I flicked the lid of the lighter open, noticing the initials 'JH' engraved faintly into the lid. It looked old, like years old, yet you could see it'd been cared for, polished and rubbed, which seemed like a really un-Daisy thing to do.

With a flick of the switch the Zippo clicked into life, a large flame bending against the wind.

'No one bothered getting me a cake,' I said with a grim smile. 'Shame really. I always liked blowing out the candles.' I thrust the cards into the flame, twisting them around until I could see that every one of them had caught fire. Blowing gently on the bundle, I walked to the end of the bench and peered into the bin, happy to see a decent amount of rubbish inside.

With a final flourish I tossed the cards into the bin and again blew gently, encouraging the flames skywards.

Daisy shifted her way along the bench, letting the warmth press against the side of her face. Pulling her legs up, she sat bundled up against the wind and turned to look at me again.

'So what are you doing for the rest of the night, then? It is your birthday after all.'

'Same as always.' I exhaled loudly. 'Probably lie on my bed and look at the stars.'

Daisy stared at me as if I was mental.

'Must be some hole in your ceiling? You should have a word with your social worker, soft lad.'

It was the first smile to pass my lips in what felt like hours, and as I explained how I'd inherited the uselcss dead stars in my room, I suddenly felt at ease. All right, it wasn't the sort of happiness I'm guessing you should feel on your birthday, but it was a start.

We sat and peered into the flames for a few minutes, until we heard the wailing of sirens. At first we ignored them, assuming they were something to do with the first of the Saturday kick-offs in one of the local pubs, but as a police car veered into view we both guessed it was paying us a visit.

'Looks like someone didn't appreciate our fire,' shouted Daisy. 'Fancy staying for a chat with the rozzers?'

'Hmmm, not really,' I replied, before turning to face the allotments. 'Legggittt!'

Turning on our heels, we took off, laughing like idiots as we ran.

CHAPTER 17

I was dizzy by the time I stumbled up the fire escape, but I couldn't decide how much of that was down to the mine-sweeping we'd done or the laughter that came afterwards.

I have to admit, I'd never even heard of sweeping until we arrived outside the Hop Pole. We'd legged it through the allotments and down the bypass for a good few minutes, until we were sure that we'd lost the rozzers, so the pub was a welcome sight. The Hop Pole was a big old boozer that sat on the corner of the bypass and was always bragging from some banner or other that they served the cheapest steak and chips in town. Hardly an advert for good grub, but the car park was never empty.

'Perfect,' Daisy said, laughing, as she saw the large group of people huddled in the doorway. 'Fancy a birthday drink?'

'Yeah, cos that's going to happen, isn't it? Come on. Let's get to the offie and nick a bottle of something.'

'No need, Billy. This one's on me.'

Smirking, she pulled me to one side and taught me the rules of sweeping. The most important being, never get greedy.

It was only ever one sweep per pub. Never more. The rest

was simple. It was all about diversions and teamwork. And man, was she a player. A joy to watch. And she was right, it was so simple.

All she did was wait until a group of drinkers, usually fellas, came outside for a smoke.

She'd watch as they approached one of the picnic tables, but it wasn't until every one of them had put their pints on the table that she'd make her move. She'd amble up to them and strike up this act. Part vulnerable and girly, part mischievous. Sometimes she'd wander up and ask for something as simple as a light; sometimes she'd start pumping them for directions. But whatever tack she took, she always got their full attention. All of them, even if there was half a dozen.

It was amazing to watch, so much so that the first time I forgot my cue. My bit was just as easy: while she was chatting away, I just had to slip up behind them and sweep a pint from the table. Only a pint, mind, never more. Not even two. Any more might arouse suspicion too quickly, whereas with one missing pint, they merely thought they'd left it inside.

By the time they were back by the electric fire, we were long gone, on to the next pub, pint glass in hand.

Three pints in and I was well away, especially as I'd barely eaten a thing all day.

If anything, I found it difficult to keep up with her, and more so when she started swiping spirits as well as beers. I forced the first vodka down with difficulty, much to her amusement. But when she appeared with a neat whisky in her hand, I felt the fear in me rise.

'Get that down you,' she said, and smiled, ramming the glass under my nose.

The smell of it alone burned at my throat, taking me back ten years. Back to a place I didn't want to be. Back to Shaun, his angry face and angrier blows.

Instinctively, I swiped at the glass, sending it flying across the beer garden, where it shattered, attracting disapproving glares from other drinkers.

Daisy grinned, thinking I was drunk rather than terrified. 'Ooops. Time we were going. Drink up.'

I necked the rest of my lager, more in desperation than anything, as I tried to wash the smell of the whisky away. The last dregs fell down my shirt as Daisy pulled me through the gate and out on to the street.

I could feel my balance leaving me as I stumbled along. 'What time is it?'

'Nearly eight o'clock.'

'I'm going to have to go.'

She looked put out. 'What do you mean, you lightweight? It's only early.'

'It's the twins. They'll be back, wondering where I am.'

'But it's your birthday. Live a bit. They'll be all right. It's only one night.'

I smiled, wishing it were that easy. 'That'd be one night too many, though. I can't let anyone else put them to bed. It's my job.'

'You're a top man, Billy Finn. Screwed up, obviously. But a top man anyway. Don't let them tell you otherwise.'

Sparking up another rollie, she walked away.

'I'll give you a buzz tomorrow,' I yelled after her, wondering if I'd hacked her off by ducking out so early.

She turned back to me with a grin and a nod, before walking on again. Lost in her own head.

I checked the time, before making a dash for home.

After checking the coast was clear, I pulled myself in through the fire escape window and into my room.

The room smelt a bit of bacon and I wondered if I should bother taking the plate downstairs. It all seemed a bit too much like hard work, so I tipped the leftovers out of the window and left the plate on the windowsill, reckoning the rain would wash it clean soon enough.

Dumping my jacket on the floor, I noticed a note folded on top of my bed.

As I bent to pick it up, a key fell from inside it. Looked like it fitted some small lock or something. Picking it up from the floor, I read the note:

> Bill,
> I just wanted to tell you I'm sorry. I got it wrong today.
> This key is for you. It unlocks the door to the old garage.
> Happy birthday, mate.
> Ronnie

I turned the key over in my hand, clueless as to what it all meant. But I was intrigued.

Before I had chance to check it out, there was a commotion in the hallway. Loud shouting voices, and one of them belonged to Lizzie.

'Get off me, will you!' she yelled. 'You can't touch me. I'll have you done!'

I dashed through the door, to be confronted by a red-faced Lizzie being tugged towards the bathroom door. It was Maggie, one of the senior scummers in the house, doing the pulling.

'Take your hands off her,' I shouted, as I took hold of Maggie's wrist. 'Take your hands off and walk away.'

My appearance seemed to take them both by surprise and Maggie let go instantly. Not that I did. I wanted her to remember not to lay a hand on Lizzie again.

She didn't like that of course and rounded on me in the predictable scummer way, with a threat of her own.

'Billy, let go of my arm right now. Lizzie had refused numerous requests to get in the bath. I was merely escorting her to the bathroom. There's no need for you to take that as an opportunity for aggression.'

But I wasn't ready to let go yet, mainly because I could see it getting to her.

'Billy, let my arm GO.'

I wasn't budging.

'Let my arm go NOW, or I will –'

'What?' I interrupted. 'You'll do what? Take the twins away from me? Bit late to threaten that one now, isn't it?'

As soon as the words were out of my mouth I regretted it, as I could feel Lizzie's gaze upon me.

'What do you mean, Bill?' she asked, a look of fear on her face. 'Where are they sending us?'

I dropped Maggie's arm. 'Nowhere, matey, nowhere. I'm just being daft. Ignore me.'

'But you just said they were sending us away. Don't let them do that, Bill. We don't want to go anywhere.'

I wrapped my arm protectively around her as I tried to calm her down. But I couldn't lie to her. Not like they'd lied to me.

'It's OK,' I repeated. 'Just get in the bath and we'll talk about it later.'

'Do you promise?'

'Of course I do. As soon as you're ready for bed we can talk about it.'

She still looked concerned as she turned towards the bathroom.

'Billy. Will you sit . . .?'

'Don't worry, Lizzie. I'll be right outside the door.'

The sad smile left my face as soon as she locked the door.

There I was, half-cut, desperately trying to think of a way of telling my only family that they were being taken elsewhere.

It would have been the perfect end to a lifer's birthday, but there was more to come.

CHAPTER 18

The walk across the lawn did me good. The wind was starting to bite, which was fine, because it blew the clouds away for a second, giving me a glimpse of the sky beyond. I breathed it in, and tried to reassure myself that the twins understood what I'd told them.

It was the quickest bath Lizzie had ever had. 'A lick and a promise', that's what Jan and Grant would have called it.

Within ten minutes, both her and Louie were sitting on the edge of their beds, waiting for me to spell it out for them. And as I began to speak, I still had no idea what I was going to say.

'Don't look so scared, you two. This isn't bad news. It's all good.' But as hard as I smiled, I felt something break as the words came out. 'They're not looking to take you away. They're trying to get you home.'

I hoped they'd understand without me spelling it out, but they didn't of course. And why would they? This was all they knew. This was home.

'To Annie's house,' I said slowly. 'Annie wants you to go and live with her.'

In that moment, all the tension fell from Lizzie's face as

she flew across the room and into my arms. Louie, on the other hand, remained on the bed, fear still scratched upon his face.

'What about you, Bill?' he said.

'Don't worry about me, mate,' I answered, as I beckoned him over.

'Bill's coming with us. Aren't you, Bill?' Lizzie butted in.

'I'm not, no. It wouldn't work. Annie's been trying hard to be well again. But she's still nervy, you know. She needs to take it slowly, make sure she can handle the two of you.'

'But once we're home and she's OK, then she'll send for you, won't she?' Lizzie asked, her grip on my arm tightening.

'Listen. It's no good thinking like that. It could be a long while until she's well enough. And by then I'll be out of here. Have my own place. A flat with rooms for both of you, so you can come at weekends and that. Whenever you want.' I couldn't believe I was saying it, but I knew I had to, no matter how much it hurt.

'But I want you to come with us, Billy. They can't split us up. You're my brother.'

'And that won't change. And I won't let you go unless I'm sure Annie can cope with it.'

The questions continued as I tucked them into their beds, and I tried as hard as I could to make it all seem positive. What good would it do to badmouth Annie now? It was a done deal and I had to make this as easy for them as I could.

Stories read, I made for the door and my usual position, only to be called back by Louie.

'Bill, don't sit outside tonight. Can't you stay in here?'

'All right,' I said, and smiled, returning to stroke his head.

I slid down the wall between their beds and rested my eyes, hoping it would encourage them to do the same.

For all the fear in the room, it didn't take them long to go to sleep. Louie fought it for a while, forcing his eyes open as he checked I was still there, but within fifteen minutes they had both caved in. I stayed a little bit longer, worrying about how many more nights I'd have like this.

As I left their room I remembered Ronnie's key in my pocket, and because I knew there was no way I was going to sleep, I crept down the stairs and out across the grounds.

Stood at the garage door, key in hand, I thought for a second about what might be inside and whether I wanted anything to do with it. This was Ronnie's gift to me after all, bought out of guilt. After a minute's hesitation, I thrust the key into the lock and turned it. I could always flog whatever was in there. It was mine after all.

It was pitch black inside, and damp. And there was a whiff of paint as well.

I ran my hand along the wall until I found the switch, and as the light flickered on, it took me a minute to work out what I was looking at.

The knackered old garage had been transformed. Each wall was painted a different colour: grey, red, white and blue. All the junk that used to litter the place had gone and the floor had been swept and painted too. All apart from a square piece in the middle that had been covered with a large blue mat.

Dotted around the room were pieces of equipment, and I groaned as I realized what I was looking at: a gym. The Colonel had built a boxing gym. I shook my head in disbelief as our past conversations popped into my head. He really thought that giving me something to hit was the answer. Well, unless the punchbag was shaped like him, that wasn't going to work.

I walked from corner to corner, checking out the stuff he'd put in there. Not all of it was new, but a lot was. There was a huge punchbag, hanging from thick chains that wrapped around the beams, a skipping rope, dumb-bells and a small round punchball that had thick elastic shooting out of the top and bottom of it. The elastic ran to the ceiling and floor, and as I aimed a punch at the ball, it zipped away from me before whipping back and whacking me in the face.

I rubbed at my nose and looked over my shoulder self-consciously. I flicked at the ball again, gently this time, and watched as the elastic shook the ball back and forth.

Nose stinging, I turned to the big punchbag, confident that it wouldn't be able to hurt me in the same way. It was huge, practically the size of me, and as I pushed it away, I could hear the chains creak against the beams above. The bag swung, and as it reached me, I launched a punch at it with my right hand. The bag thudded against my fist, sending a shock of pain shooting through my knuckles, past my wrist and up my arm. I swore and stumbled away from the bag, the pain in my arm competing with the throbbing of my nose.

'That's what gloves are for,' came a voice from behind me.

I turned, to see Ronnie stood in the doorway.

'You'll break your fist punching it like that.'

'No, really?' I moaned, tucking my hand under my armpit

to try and numb the pain. I didn't have the coordination to cup a hand to my nose as well.

'So what do you think?' he crowed as he strode into the room. 'Do you like it?'

I stared him down as he stopped in front of me, grabbing the bag as it swung slowly between us.

'Like *what*?'

'Your gym. I've been working on it for weeks.'

'Well, you've wasted your time. I don't want this. I'm not interested in boxing.'

I pushed the bag into his belly and walked towards the door.

'That's not what you've said before.'

I stopped and looked back, confused by what he'd said. 'You what?'

'When we spoke about boxing before. You were interested enough then.'

I shook my head in irritation, unable to let his comment slide. 'You really do talk out of your arse, you know that?'

'I don't think so, Bill. When we spoke about it before, you said you'd do it if you could spar with me.'

I couldn't help but laugh. 'Yeah, and that's going to happen, isn't it?'

'Absolutely,' he replied, with no trace of a smile on his face.

I watched as he walked slowly to a metal trunk in the far corner of the room. And as much as I wanted to turn around and walk out, I couldn't help but stay.

After a bit of a wait, he stood up from the trunk, holding what looked like a huge brown leather cushion.

'Well, here it is, my friend. The moment you've waited for for years. Your chance to hit me with my permission.'

I looked at him, baffled. But before I could say a word, he lifted the cushion up above his head. Putting his head through a hole, he pulled the padding down past his chest, until it covered his upper body. He looked like he was wearing one of those comedy sumo outfits you see at the fair.

'This,' he said, smiling as he saw the bemusement on my face, 'is body armour. A trainer's best friend. And now yours too.'

He tossed me a pair of gloves.

'There is just one rule to this, Billy,' he barked, as he pulled big cushioned mitts on to his fists. 'You only punch where there's padding. You understand me?'

I couldn't quite get my head around what was going on. Here I was, with an invitation to lay into the person I wanted to punch more than anyone in the world. Well, almost. But for some reason I couldn't go for it.

'I don't get it,' I said, with a shake of my head. 'I don't understand what this is. You want me to punch you . . . That bit, I understand. What I don't get is why?'

'Because you're angry. And you have been ever since I've known you, which is half your life.'

'Don't I know it,' I muttered under my breath.

'I don't blame you for being angry. I get angry and I've never had to live anywhere but with my family. So I can't even imagine how you feel. What I do know is that this helped me a long time ago. And to be honest, I don't know what else to try. I'm out of ideas. So this is it. This is your chance. It's up to you.'

'So I hit you. That's it?'

'Wherever there's padding or a glove,' he said, and nodded.

'And what about a bell?' I asked, knowing there had to be a catch somewhere in it all.

'There's no bell in this, Billy. You just keep swinging until you're done.'

I couldn't believe what I was hearing. Couldn't believe he thought I'd punch myself out before he was left on the floor.

'You're kidding?'

'Don't flatter yourself, Bill. I've faced bigger than you, believe me. So let's have it. No pad, no punch. Otherwise, anything goes.'

Lifting his gloved hands in front of him, he braced himself for the onslaught.

CHAPTER 19

Maybe it was the beers I'd necked earlier in the evening, but I was struggling to get my head around the sight in front of me. I'd dreamed of having a free shot at Ronnie for years and here he was, standing in front of me, telling me to do it.

Pulling the second glove on to my fist, I told myself to stop thinking about it and enjoy the moment. After all, it was my birthday.

I turned to face him and sized up the area I had to play with. He wasn't small to start with, but kitted out in his body armour he looked mountainous. I studied the options carefully, planning where I was going to start.

'Come on, then, Billy. Show us what you've got.' He smiled, mitts held at chin level.

I lifted my fists until they were cocked like pistols, ready to fire. Putting the weight on to my front foot, I let fly with a right hand that smacked into his glove.

It felt good.

'Not bad,' he said, grinning, 'but try standing with your legs further apart. It'll help you balance better and punch harder.'

But what he didn't understand was that this wasn't about technique. This was about revenge. I flicked out another left jab, followed by another and another.

He just soaked it up and shuffled to his left, forcing me to turn with him.

Keeping my eye on his mitts, I decided to step up the pace, and for the first time started to jab with both hands. Sometimes a quick one-two, sometimes a flurry of fists. It wasn't pretty, but with each impact I felt my heartbeat leap and the adrenalin pump further around my body. I stepped up the pace again, but this time I was beginning to move him around instead, and I could see the colour start to rise in his face, the sweat breaking for freedom across his forehead.

I kept my gaze fixed on his. I wanted him to see me snarling, to see the pleasure I was getting from pounding his fists. But as my rhythm built, so did his. It was as if he was anticipating my every punch or, worse still, that he was actually showing me where to land each blow.

Desperate to gain the upper hand, I decided it was time to shift to the body. So, as I bent my right shoulder and pretended to snap another punch into his mitt, I shifted my weight and threw a swinging left that caught him flush in the kidneys.

As my fist slammed into the armour, I saw surprise on his face for the first time, and as he stumbled backwards, trying to regain his balance, I followed up with a big right to the other side of his body.

I thought for a second that the blow would floor him, but if anything it stirred him up a bit and, despite the sweat pouring from his face, he couldn't suppress a smile.

'I like it, Bill, I like it. Didn't see that one coming. Come on. Don't stop there. Let's see what you've got!'

I didn't need a second invitation and ploughed forward, pulling my head down into my chest as I let a flurry of wild left and right hooks rip into his body. With his elbows tucked into his chest and his mitts covering his face, he grunted and groaned, but showed no sign of calling an end to it all. He just stood there, soaking up the blows.

He wasn't the only one starting to feel the pain of it all. My breathing was quick and ragged, but I couldn't entertain the idea of stopping. I could feel the anger feeding its way into my fists, and it was coming so thick and fast that it wasn't just the Colonel I was hitting any more. It was so many people. All the social workers who'd let me down, the teachers who'd ridiculed me, the scummers who'd promised so much before leaving for other jobs.

Faces flashed before my eyes. And for every face there was an incident, a memory, a time that they had let me down. Each punch that landed was revenge, my chance to tell them that I hadn't forgotten what they did.

But as the punches added up and the faces changed, there was one person who kept coming back, no matter how many times I hit him.

Shaun.

I jabbed and hooked, and pushed and shoved, but no matter how many blows I landed, I couldn't shake him from my head, couldn't forget the punches he'd landed on me.

My fists were pounding and my arms were knackered, but I couldn't stop swinging. Not while he was still in my head. So I threw and threw and threw, until my lungs were burning. My balance was shot and, as I rocked backwards and forwards, I half expected to fall. But I wouldn't let myself. Not until his face had gone from my head.

My work rate was slowing, and the punches were landing lower and lower on Ronnie's armour. The snap of my blows turned into slaps, and I could barely see as the sweat was blinding me. I had no idea how long I had been stood there. In fact, the only thing I did know was that the Colonel was still in front of me, taking every blow I had.

His breathing was as quick as mine, and his face the unhealthiest red, but still he beckoned me forward, and as Shaun's face glowed in my head, I had no option but to carry on.

But then everything shifted. My knees seemed to buckle and I stumbled forward. As I fell, I could still see him, laughing, snarling and screaming, and as I tumbled into the Colonel, I had to throw one last punch, in the vain hope of banishing him for good. It landed on Ron's right hand, then slipped past his arm and around his back. My other arm reached forward in the same way, and before I knew it I was slumped in his arms, gasping for air.

I don't know why he did it, whether it was out of affection or merely to hold me up, but I felt his arms grip me hard around my waist. What I did know was that for the first time in eight years, I didn't instantly try to shrug him off.

CHAPTER 20

Waking in the night is something I'm used to. Waking in the night barely able to move my arms or legs was a new sensation. It felt like someone had crept in and pinned me to my mattress while I was sleeping.

Groaning, I grabbed the edge of my bed and heaved myself on to my side, every bit of my body screaming its objection. For a minute or two, I was actually scared, thought I'd had a stroke or something, until I realized that that doesn't tend to happen to people aged fifteen years and one day. I flexed my arm up to my shoulder, trying to coax some blood into it, and wondered how many punches I must have actually thrown to feel so stiff and sore.

It had taken me a good ten minutes to stand up again after falling on top of Ron, and he wasn't in such great shape himself. Still, he managed to help me with my gloves before telling me to lie on the mat with my hands above my head, and as the air poured into my mouth, I felt oddly alive.

The garage was hot, despite the late hour, and I watched, grinning, as Ronnie struggled to yank the body armour back over his head. As he pulled, his T-shirt came up with it, leaving his back exposed. From the colour of his raw-looking skin, it was obvious he'd felt a lot of the punches I'd thrown, regardless of the padding, but more baffling were the scars that littered his back. Long jagged lines were etched in rows, pretty much from shoulder to shoulder, and though they were faded, they still looked angry.

As the armour fell to the mat with a thud, he clocked what I was looking at and, with a bit of a struggle, managed to pull his shirt down again. Wiping away the sweat that poured off his forehead, he slumped to the floor next to me, lifting his arms above his head. God knows what we must have looked like, apart from a complete car wreck.

'Well, that's got the heart beating,' he groaned, brushing his sleeve across his face. 'Feels good, doesn't it?'

'Suppose so, yeah.'

'Your hands all right? They'll probably be a bit sore in the morning. If I'd thought you were going to punch me for so long, I'd have strapped them up first.'

'They're fine. Strangely enough, punching you doesn't hurt at all,' I lied.

'Yeah, weird. Who'd have thought it?'

Ronnie paused before asking the next question, and I could hear the nerves in his voice as the words came out.

'So what do you make of it, then? The gym? It's yours. My present to you.'

The question felt loaded, and although he'd just let me batter him for the best part of ten minutes, he didn't deserve a load of praise.

'It's all right, yeah. Can't say it's what I wanted, but it has its advantages, I suppose.'

Silence set in as we tried to catch our breath, but it felt uncomfortable, so I chose to break it.

'Did it take you long? To put it all together?'

He looked taken aback that I'd even asked, but jumped at the chance of a conversation.

'Been about five weeks, I suppose. I've been wanting to do it for a long time, but I was convinced you wouldn't buy into it.'

My only response was a huff. I wanted him to see he was right.

'But then your review happened and, to be honest, after what had gone on in there, and with the things we were insisting you do – well, I just decided that you'd be needing this more than ever. Needing some way of blowing off steam. It was either this or watch you explode . . . and I didn't fancy cleaning up that sort of mess.'

I sat silently, letting his words sink in. As much as I hated to admit it, he had put a shed-load of work into it.

'So where's all the gear from? You been flogging the wife's jewellery or something?'

'Not exactly.' He laughed. 'I had a load of stuff cluttering up my garage at home. Just decided it was time to get it all on eBay and put the money to better use. Some of the stuff is new – the speedball, the skipping ropes and that – but a lot of it is second-hand or reconditioned. Some of it belonged to my boys. But now they're not home any more it seemed daft hanging on to it.' His voice tailed off for a second, before he pulled himself to his feet and busied himself in his normal fashion.

I looked around the garage, trying to work out which

stuff was new and which had been his sons', but to be honest I didn't really care. I was just trying to get my head around the fact that it was mine. It was a sensation I wasn't used to.

'Listen, Bill. I'm not going to make you use this place. That's got to be your choice. But it's yours and yours alone. There are two keys. The one you have and a spare that'll stay in the house in case you lose yours. If you want to use it on your own that's fine, but I'm happy to join in. Although,' he added with a wince as he rubbed his gut, 'you might need to give me a day or two to recover.'

He pulled himself to his feet and staggered towards the door.

'Don't stay out here too long or you'll freeze. Oh, and I'd warm down if I was you, otherwise you'll be aching in the morning.'

Of course I completely ignored him, and just lay there for another ten minutes, before locking the garage carefully and stumbling back to the house. I'd wondered about a shower, then thought better of it, preferring instead to collapse into bed.

It still took me a long time to get to sleep, but perhaps not as long as usual, and when I woke, stiff as a board, I could see from my phone that four hours had passed. Again, it was unusual for me to sleep for such a long stretch.

I spent the next half-hour or so trying to ease some life back into my arms, but despite all the rubbing and flexing they continued to yell their irritation at me.

My mind was fixed on the gym, and the work that must have gone on in getting it ready, and to my annoyance I couldn't see how Ron had found the time to do it. He spent every minute of his shift bossing around the other scummers and lifers in the house, so it wasn't as if he was shirking there. The only things I could think of were that he was talking out of his arse and that someone else had done the work, or that he'd done it outside of work time.

I balanced the two options in my head. Fobbing someone else's work off as his own was a possibility, but I just couldn't believe it. I'd seen the pride in his eyes as he'd talked about it.

I shook my head in irritation at the fact that I was even giving this head space. So what if he'd spent a bit of his own time giving a room a lick of paint? It was his choice, and he was only doing it out of guilt in the first place.

I argued the toss with myself for a good few minutes, and probably would have still been doing it had the door not creaked slowly open. Forgetting my aching body, I zipped to my feet in a flash, ready to have a pop at whoever was on the way in, only to be confronted by the sight of a teary-looking Louie.

'Hey, mate,' I whispered, stroking his head.

'I woke up and you weren't there,' he cried. 'I don't want to be in there tonight. Can I sleep in here instead?'

It was a question that needed no answer, so he stumbled to the mattress and under my duvet.

Climbing carefully over, I pulled myself under the covers beside him, and felt all my aches fade away as he nestled closer to me, tucking his body against my stomach.

It took him seconds to find sleep mode, which gave me joy and broke my heart in the same breath. I knew he needed me, but at the same time I knew he'd soon have Annie instead.

I pushed the thought to the back of my head and, as hard as I fought it, had no option but to give in to sleep.

CHAPTER 21

The sun was bursting through the curtains by the time I woke up, my arms complaining even more loudly about the pounding I'd given them.

I tried to roll on to my back and stretch out, but couldn't. Something was wedged up behind me, and with Louie still snoring against my chest, I was properly stuck.

I craned my neck as far as my aches would allow, trying to work out what on earth was going on behind me, but all I could see was a lump in the duvet, rising and falling slowly.

Clenching every muscle I had, I heaved myself upright and lifted the covers, to find Lizzie there, curled up in a ball. It was like someone had put a mirror in between her and Louie. I was clueless as to when that had happened. I certainly hadn't woken up when she'd wandered in, and instantly I felt guilty that she had needed me and I hadn't even known.

I sat on the bed for a bit, watching them, jealous at their ability to sleep. The only time I'd found any peace lately had been that night at Jan and Grant's, and as my mind wandered, I started to hatch a plan about when I could make a return visit.

The twins snored on and eight thirty ticked around. As it was Sunday, none of the scummers were in a rush to wake the troops, not at the expense of an extra hour in their beds.

The silence was broken by the buzzing of my phone, although I had no idea who'd be texting me at this time of the morning.

```
Am gssng u r up? Meet me usual plce,
11.30. Dx
```

A grin flicked across my face as the rest of the day took a turn for the better.

Pulling myself to my feet, I went in search of clothes – in particular, ones that had been washed at some point in the last six months.

To be honest, everything I put my nose to had the same stale whiff to it, which confused me. There must be something on the floor that hadn't been worn yet . . .

It wasn't until I lifted my arm and stood downwind of my pits that I realized maybe the problem wasn't so much the clothes but the body that was about to fill them.

Pulling a towel from the back of the door, I headed for the shower. If I could get myself clean, I could cover the smell of my clothes with a blast of Lynx. Closing the bedroom door gently behind me, I couldn't help but smile. What was coming over me?

I spent the walk to the bench worrying I was going to be stupidly late. The state of my body meant everything had taken three times as long as it normally did. So when the can of deodorant had decided to hide from me as well, I was seriously behind time. As I reached the bypass, I tried to break into a gentle jog, but it was a short-lived attempt. Every bend of the elbow and jolt of the knee sent shock-waves up to my brain.

As I reached the corner that led to the allotment, I could see I was nearly thirty minutes late. It was pretty unlikely Daisy would still be waiting. She wasn't exactly full of patience.

So it came as a bit of a relief to be greeted by a cloud of cigarette smoke hovering above the bench. Daisy was in residence, and if the grin on her face was anything to go by, she was in good form too.

'What happened to you last night, then?' she asked, the sentence peppered with laughter.

'Nothing. Why?' I answered defensively.

'Because you're walking like you've crapped yourself . . . and what is that smell? Good God, Bill, have you had a bath in a bucket full of bog cleaner or something?'

'Is this what you wanted to see me for, just to rip the piss?' I huffed, as I rethought my plan to sit beside her on the bench.

'I'm sorry,' she said, giggling. 'I've just never seen anyone walk like that . . . unless they had piles or something.' She was off again, her shoulders shaking beneath her oversized shirt.

My temper rising, I couldn't help but bite on the bait, and before I knew it the words had escaped from my mouth.

'You can talk. You get dressed in the dark this morning?

I see you're wearing your dad's shirt again. Who was your old man anyway? Some kind of giant or something?'

The words hung in the air as the smile disappeared from Daisy's face. She jammed the rollie back into her mouth and sparked it up again, inhaling deeply.

'I'm sorry, Daisy,' I moaned. 'I didn't think.'

'It's all right,' she said, her face impassive. 'I had that one coming, so forget about it. So, what *did* happen last night? You look like you're hurting.'

'I'm all right. It just didn't turn out quite how I thought it would when I left you.'

And then I told her the story of the night before, from my conversation with the twins, to the gym and my 'fight' with Ron, right through to my visitors during the night.

'Sounds like you had a proper birthday after all,' she said with a grin. 'And what's that Ronnie all about? He's a dark horse, that one.'

'What do you mean?'

'Well, you go on about him all the time, about what a nightmare he is, and how he treats you badly and all that. Next thing you know, he's flogged half of his worldly goods to make you the next champion of the world! He sounds like a real nightmare to me, Bill, he really does.'

I couldn't help but feel defensive as the sarcasm dripped off her words.

'You don't know what he's like, Daisy. He's manipulative. You don't get anything for nothing with Ron. He doesn't work like that.'

'You need to cut him a little bit of slack. I know he's a pain in the arse. I can see that from all the things you've told me. But answer me this. Aside from the twins, who have you known the longest in your life? Who's been there, without fail, regardless of whether you wanted them around or not?'

'Dunno,' I mumbled as I kicked the bench like a sulking kid. 'Social worker, I suppose.'

'Billy!' she shouted, impatience filling her voice. 'That's crap and you know it. Just admit it. It won't kill you to say Ronnie's name, you know.'

'Whatever.' I was determined not to say the words. 'You up for doing something, then? Or do you just want to take the mick all day?'

Daisy bumped me with her shoulder, her attempt to break the ice and move the conversation on.

'Nah, I'm done. You're too easy to wind up. Anyway, I've got something for you.'

My ears pricked up. 'Oh aye, what's that?'

'Close your eyes and hold out your hand.'

I looked at her suspiciously. 'I'm not ten.'

'I know you're not. But if you want your prezzie, then do as I say.'

Frowning, I did as she asked and felt her drop something on to my palm.

'What's this?' I asked, opening my eyes to a small maroon box.

'What does it look like?'

'Looks like a box.'

'You scare me sometimes, Bill, you really do.'

'It's a ring box, isn't it?' A bit of fear had crept into my voice.

'Depends what's in it, doesn't it?'

'And what *is* in it?'

'Well, open it, you tool, and then you'll know. And don't look so scared. It's not what you think it is. Don't flatter yourself.'

I looked her in the eyes as I flipped the box open. I couldn't help but think it was just another of her wind-ups. And if it was, I was off.

She was right, though. It wasn't what I thought. In fact, at first I was a bit disappointed, because wedged inside the box was a jagged piece of green plastic.

I frowned as I brought it closer to my face. 'What is it, then?'

'Take it out of the box and you'll see.'

I wedged my fingers in and pulled it out, letting it fall into my hand.

It was a star. A green plastic star. And for a second I was speechless.

'Thought it might be just what you needed. Twenty-four-carat plastic, you know. Not just any old crap. Guaranteed to glow in the dark, that is!'

'Cheers, mate.' I was smiling now, amazed that she had even remembered our conversation.

'Just don't lose it, all right? I can't afford another one.'

'Reckon I'll be needing it. Can't imagine I'll be doing a lot of sleeping once the twins have gone.'

'You mustn't think like that. There's still a lot that could happen, and from what you've told me, Annie sounds pretty flaky. Any sign of that this time and there's no way they'll let it happen.'

'You know what scares me most?' I admitted as I sat myself on the back of the bench.

Daisy shook her head.

'That they'll forget about me.'

'Don't be an idiot, Bill. There's no way that that's going to happen. You're their brother. You've practically brought them up.'

'But you haven't seen them when they're around her. I can't compete. They only see her once a week and it's like I'm invisible. What's it going to be like once they're living with her?'

'Look,' she said, sitting beside me. 'Someone I know told me that you've got to fight stupid thoughts with logic. To prove to yourself that whatever you're thinking is nonsense.'

I just looked at her blankly, clueless as to what she was banging on about.

'I'm serious, Bill. I mean, what happened to the twins when you went to live with that foster family?'

I tensed at the mention of Jan and Grant, and started picking at some loose skin by my thumb.

'Come on, Bill. I'm trying to help you here. Throw me a bone, will you?'

'What do you want to know?' I barked. 'There's nothing to tell!'

'Well, what did the twins make of it?'

'It was horrible, what do you think? They didn't understand why they couldn't come with me. They thought I was leaving them. Abandoning them, just like Annie did. When the scummers told them about it they cried for about a week, wouldn't let me out of their sight, even to go to the bog. I begged Ronnie and the social workers to keep us together, told them I didn't care about getting a placement, told them

I'd wreck the place once I got there, so the new family would have no choice but to send me back.'

'And did they listen?'

'Nah. They reckoned this was the only option. That they'd never find a family prepared to take on all three of us. But the twins as a pair, that was a different matter. They had someone lined up for them, a family who'd take them on a long-term placement.'

'But that was good, wasn't it? At least they weren't being left behind.'

'Yeah, but the problem was Annie. She didn't mind signing me over, but as soon as she got wind about the twins she changed her tune. Reckoned she was clean again, started turning up for contact, making plans to take them home for good.'

'What I'm getting at, Bill,' said Daisy gently, 'is what happened between you and the twins while you were gone. Because from what you've told me, I can't imagine that they changed towards you.'

'Course they didn't,' I said, defensive again. 'There was a load of tears and that, but they knew it wasn't my choice to leave. And I got to see them every week. They were allowed to come and spend Sundays at my house.'

'So what makes you think it'll be any different this time? You've been apart before and nothing changed. They're still your family. You've got to think about it logically. Why will it be any different *this time*?'

I bit my lip as the answer charged into my head.

Because this time they're leaving me *behind. And the difference is, Annie wants them. Jan and Grant didn't want me. Not once they realized what I was.*

There was no way I was saying that out loud, so I turned on the biggest smile I had and tried to fob her off.

'You're right. I see what you're saying. Nothing changed last time, so nothing will this time. I get it. Cheers.'

She shook her head and sighed. 'You, Billy Finn, are full of shit. And I can smell it from a mile off. Or maybe that's just your deodorant.'

I tried to butt in. But of course she had other ideas.

'Luckily for you, you have a friend who has a plan. And a camera. By the time I've finished, there's no way the twins will ever forget their big brother.'

So that was it. Discussion over. And for the first time in our conversation, I couldn't help but believe her.

CHAPTER 22

Her idea was a decent one, I suppose. Genius, Ronnie reckoned.

'Life-story books are a great idea,' he crowed, as he yanked the glove on to my fist. 'I've used them a few times when kids are moving on. Gives them something to look back on down the line. A sense of who they are and what they came from.'

'But this isn't a book, is it? She's going to record it all on film.'

'Book, film . . . makes no difference. In fact, her idea's better, because whenever the twins want to see you, all they have to do is put on the DVD. I'm sure they'd rather see your face and hear your voice than read a letter from you.'

I could see his point, and I didn't mind talking to a camera, although I didn't have a clue what I was going to say. The thing that bothered me was Daisy coming to the house. Seeing where I lived. I knew there wasn't really any other way of doing it, though. She wanted to film me walking round the place, reminding the twins of where they slept, where they ate and played. I couldn't do that on my own. And I didn't want anyone else behind the camera but her.

'What do I say, though?' I asked, as he pulled the armour over his head. 'I'm going to sound like a total plank, aren't I?'

'You know what, Bill? I wouldn't even think about it. Just say what comes into your head. Now, you ready for a round or two?'

I banged my gloves together in anticipation of working some frustration out on to his ribs. This was the third time he'd agreed to a bit of sparring and, as much as I hated to admit it, I was beginning to enjoy it. Of course he was taking it too seriously, telling me to 'widen my stance' and 'punch through the pad', but to be honest, once I was swinging, I just tuned him out. All I could focus on were the body armour and the sense of satisfaction I felt as I pummelled it. I had so many memories to put straight and each punch gave me the chance to have my own bit of revenge. The only face I couldn't banish, though, was Shaun's, and it was him that spurred me on. It didn't matter how many punches I threw, or how hard I landed them, his sneering face just wouldn't go away, and as the sessions went on I started to doubt I would ever get him out of my head.

As the minutes fizzed by, I could feel my body begin to tire and could see the Colonel flagging as well. But to his credit, he never once told me to stop. In fact, there were times I thought he knew I was thinking about Shaun, as he stepped up his encouragement, barking at me to continue.

I punched until I was unable to raise my gloves even as high as my waist. As I bent double and tried to shake Shaun from my head, the Colonel staggered backwards, tugging at the body armour as if it were on fire.

'Good grief, Bill, you punch like a mule.'

I would have laughed had I not been gasping for breath. 'I thought mules kicked?'

'Kicked, punched, what's the difference? The result's the same.'

We were silent for a while, wheezing like a couple of asthmatic old fellas gasping for breath after one fag too many.

'You enjoying it, then?' he asked finally as he warmed down.

'Don't know if enjoy's the word really. But it's all right, I suppose.'

'It's weird to watch, you know? Once you start punching, it's like Billy's gone somewhere else. I mean, what are you thinking about once you're into it?'

My mind reeled at the prospect of letting Shaun out of my head. Of the damage he could do if I let him loose anywhere but in my memories. *Not yet, not yet,* I told myself. Leave him at home with Annie. Annie, Shaun and bottles of whisky. If I kept it all together and in my head, it'd be fine.

'Nothing really. It's like you say, my head just clears and I concentrate on technique.'

Ronnie smiled, though whether he believed me was another matter.

'I'm just pleased you're getting something out of it. Means a lot to me, it does. Listen. I've got to get back to the house. There's paperwork needs doing, and a hallway to vacuum before this girlfriend of yours arrives.' Walking towards the door, he gurned some ridiculous kissing expression as he went.

I'd have told him where to go if I'd had the energy.

*

The list of things to do was endless and Daisy was arriving in less than an hour.

That morning, before boxing, I'd had a crack at working the washing machine and dryer, and as I stuck my nose into the clean clothes, I couldn't help but congratulate myself. Nothing had shrunk or dyed itself pink. All right, every bit was creased, but ironing wasn't going to happen, no matter who was coming round.

The problem I had now was what to do with the clothes. When they were filthy I had no problem scattering them all over my bedroom floor, but it seemed like a bit of a waste now they were clean. For the first time since trashing my wardrobe, I was regretting it, and had no option but to fold the clothes as best I could and pile them on my windowsill, before shutting the curtains. At least that way I could hide the boarded-up window at the same time.

After tidying my room into some sort of order, I had another shower, paying attention to go easier on the soap. I didn't fancy another ribbing from Daisy.

By the time I was dressed, there was only one thing left to do and that was have a quiet word with the rest of the lifers. Let them know that I was having a mate around and that if they gave me any grief I'd have my revenge later on. Strangely, it didn't take any of them long to catch my drift. In fact, I barely saw any of them for the rest of the day. Perfect.

Pity, then, that Ronnie didn't choose to do the same. He looked more excited than me and the twins combined, and although they would be going out with Annie for the afternoon, the Colonel was sticking around.

He was all smiles as he introduced himself to Daisy, and as I moved her swiftly away, he had the nerve to give me a wink and a sly thumbs up. Cheeky git. Like I cared what he thought.

Of course the twins thought Daisy was wicked. Her face lit up when she met them and they didn't want to leave her alone, peppering her with question after question.

'What's your name?'

'Where do you live?'

'How do you know our Billy?'

I listened carefully as she answered, hoping to pick up a bit of info that I didn't already know.

However, when Louie chirped up with, 'Are you Billy's girlfriend?' I realized it might be time to get cracking, but not before Daisy answered, 'He should be so lucky!'

'I thought you two were getting ready for Annie?' I butted in.

'She isn't coming for another hour and a half and we're ready already,' Lizzie moaned.

'Well, I've got something for you that might make the time pass a bit quicker,' Daisy said, and she pulled a DVD from her bag.

'*The Princess Bride*,' yelled Lizzie. 'Brilliant.'

'Looks like a girl's film,' mumbled Louie, unimpressed.

'You see, that's where you're wrong,' said Daisy. 'Do you like pirates, Louie?'

He nodded.

'And what about sword fights? And giants and monsters?'

Louie nodded his head so quickly it was in danger of falling off.

'Then this, my friend,' she raved, 'is the film for you. Go on. Give it a try.'

With that, Louie whipped the case out of Lizzie's hand and ran for the lounge.

'Right, then.' Daisy grinned. 'Let's get you ready for your close-up.'

I sat and stared at the red light winking at me.

'Whenever you're ready, Bill,' said Daisy softly.

I didn't have a clue where to even start, so looked around their room, hoping it might give me some inspiration.

'Er, hiya, you two. It's me, Bill.' I winced at the stupidity of how that sounded. 'I'm . . . we're . . . well, this DVD is for you. It's called your life-story book. Except we thought we'd film it instead.' I paused, ready to stop, but Daisy made this circular motion with her hand. *Keep going, keep going.*

'We thought you could take it with you when you go to live at Annie's, so you can watch it whenever you want. Just so you don't forget where you've lived and so you can see me whenever you like. Well, this is your bedroom . . .'

Daisy jerked the camera away from me and started to scan the walls instead, which made me feel tons better.

'It's been your room for eight years now, since we first arrived, although you've not always slept in these beds. You had bunk beds for a while. Do you remember? You loved them, you did. Or at least whoever had the top bunk did. Ronnie made you take it in turns each week, cos you used to fight over who got to sleep on top. You'd scrap over it nearly every night, until in the end Ron got rid of them. Reckoned it was more trouble than it was worth.'

I smiled as I remembered the tears when he swapped them for two single beds. It was like the end of the world.

'Oh, this . . .' I laughed, pointing Daisy to the wall nearest me. 'This is the gallery wall. When you were about six, all you wanted to do was draw on it. It didn't matter whether it was paint or felt tips or crayons. Whatever you could get your hands on, it went all over the wall. It used to drive the carers mad, it did. At first they'd try and paint over it, then they'd get cross and get you to join in with them, as if it was punishment or something. You didn't care. You loved it. In the end, Ronnie covered the entire wall in this blackboard paint and bought you this massive tub of chalk. You went mad for it. We used to think that sometimes you got sent to your room on purpose, just so you could go and draw all over it again.'

Daisy was grinning behind the camera, urging me on, and now I was off and running, there seemed to be loads to say.

'Do you remember which books you liked best before bed? When you were younger you loved the one about the elephant and the bad baby. I used to have to read it to you every night for about two years, till you knew it better than me. Then there was *Flat Stanley*. That was when you were older, though, and it was the first book that you wanted to read to me, especially the bit when his brother blew him up again with the bike pump. Always made us laugh, that did. I hope you're still reading books at Annie's house too.'

Daisy gave me a big thumbs up.

'And don't let her forget to tuck the duvet under your feet before you go to sleep, otherwise your feet'll get really cold.

I used to let you go to sleep in your socks, until Ronnie told you your feet wouldn't grow if you wore them in bed!'

The red light blinked off and Daisy let the camera fall to her side.

'Wicked, Bill, wicked. I reckon that'll do for in here. Where do you want to go next?'

Now we were off and flying, I didn't feel so much of a dick and we spent the next hour or so moving round the house, from kitchen to hallway to dining room, even the scummers' office as well. My confidence grew with every room, and along with that came a sense that maybe this would work after all. At least, until the Colonel jumped in.

'Any chance of me leaving a message on that, Daisy?' he asked as we stood in his office.

Daisy flicked me a look asking for approval, and when I shrugged, she just said, 'Sure.'

'I'll check on the twins,' I said, getting out before I was forced to sit in on what would be a long and dull speech.

I sat in the lounge with them for a few minutes, not that they knew I was there. They were completely lost in the film, which did look pretty good, and it certainly wasn't a girl's film, as Louie had thought. It was all sword fights and duels and funny one-liners, but with enough princesses to keep Lizzie happy as well. By the time I knew what was happening I'd been sucked in too, and as the credits rolled, the twins returned reluctantly to the room as if from a trance.

'That was corking,' said Louie, stretching his arms like he'd been the one with the sword in his hand, not the masked hero. 'Can we watch it again later?'

'You'll have to ask Daisy if you can borrow it,' I replied,

although I knew what the answer would be. 'Why don't you get your shoes on? Annie's due any minute.'

With that, they tore out of the door and up the stairs, imaginary swords in hands, leaving me with an empty room. Something I'd have to get used to, I suppose.

Twenty minutes later and the house was quieter still. Annie had been and gone, the twins galloping behind her, doubly excited as they were allowed to spend the day with her on their own. No scummers to spoil their fun – the days of supervised contact were gone, another nail hammered firmly into my coffin.

Daisy watched from the door as they disappeared through the gate, before jabbing me in the arm.

'Come on, then. Stop looking morbid. We've got more filming to finish before they get back.'

'Can't we leave it as it is? I haven't got anything left to say,' I moaned, the frustration biting hard inside me.

'Can do if you want the last thing they see on screen to be Ronnie,' she replied, knowing full well that it wasn't.

'One more shot, then, and that's it.'

'Perfect,' she said, grinning, then pushed me down the steps and on to the grounds by the house. She marched me over to the bench by the garage, before giving me a pep talk about what she wanted.

'Now remember, this is the last shot. The thing they'll remember most once they turn it off. So keep it punchy and tell them the truth.'

'What do you mean "the truth"?'

'I don't know, Bill. They're your family, not mine!' She took a deep breath. 'Look, there are so many things I wish I'd said to my mum and dad. Things I never got chance to. Things I regret now. Well, you've got the chance, so don't waste it.'

She pushed the button without pausing. We were rolling.

'Hiya. It's me again. Hope Ronnie didn't bore you to death. I'm sat here on the bench in the garden and I don't think there's much more to show you.' I paused and looked around, desperate for some inspiration. 'We used to sit out here a lot in the summer. Hey, do you remember the day we sat here and read *The Twits* from start to finish? Louie got so obsessed with it that he tried to hide food in his hair like Mr Twit. We were picking dried cornflakes out of it for days.'

I grinned like a fool at the memory, before realizing I really had run out of things to say.

'I hope you like this. It was Daisy's idea, to be honest.' Daisy spun the camera round to face her and waved before whipping it back to me. 'But we've enjoyed making it. It reminded me a bit that it hasn't all been rubbish living here. Most of it has, but not all.'

I looked down the lens of the camera, my mind an absolute blank.

'I don't know what else to say really, except enjoy being at home. You're in the right place, you know? It was never right you being here. You deserve better. So enjoy it, and don't forget, if ever you need me, for anything, doesn't matter what time of day it is, you can call me. Just because we're not under the same roof, it doesn't mean anything changes. I'm still your brother. See you soon.'

And with a wave, I stood up from the bench and the camera went to sleep.

CHAPTER 23

The car was so full of crap by the time we left home that I thought we'd spend most of the journey hot-rodding along the motorway on the back wheels.

For a man who'd spent weeks roughing it outdoors with his army cronies, the Colonel was hell-bent on taking a load of gear for only two nights' camping.

'Best to be prepared,' he'd said with a smug grin. 'After all, a failure to plan is a plan to failure.'

Me and Lizzie stared at him, bemused, while Louie flashed a 'loser' sign at him with his thumb and finger. I don't think Ronnie had a clue what Lou was on about, but he knew it wasn't a compliment.

The first weeks of summer had passed in a flash and school was starting to beckon, playing on my mind. We were all pretty excited by the trip, though. Any time spent away from home and the other lifers, even if it was a trip to the shops, was a bonus, but to get two nights away . . . well, it just didn't happen.

'You deserve it, all three of you. You've had a lot to deal with lately and we wanted to give you the chance to spend some family time together.'

I felt a stab of sadness in my gut. If this was our last holiday before being split again, I knew I couldn't spend the whole trip kicking up. I wanted the twins to leave with only good memories of me, and selfishly I wanted some of my own.

So I bit my tongue as Ronnie piled the boot high with supplies, even when he talked us through every bit of kit that went in. It was only when the boot slammed shut that he let us get in.

Maggie, the other scummer coming with us, couldn't resist ribbing him either as she clambered in beside the twins.

'Well, that was great fun, Ron, it really was, but we'd better start getting all the luggage back in the house, hadn't we? I think I've reached my retirement date. I wouldn't mind, but I was only forty-five when this shift started.'

'Oh, you may laugh, but you'll thank me for my planning if the weather turns.'

'I'll thank you more if we manage to pitch the tents before the sun disappears, so get your foot down, will you?'

I felt him bristling beside me, but could tell he was trying to keep a lid on it, and by the time we'd reached the motorway, he was properly cheerful. So cheerful that he allowed the twins to put one of their CDs on, despite their appalling taste in music.

You couldn't blame them – they were still so young after all – but with every sugar-coated pop song that burst through the speakers, they would pogo in their seats, tipping the car further and further back. Lou got so into it, he started drumming on the back of Ronnie's headrest. I sat and watched his reaction, expecting him to bark at Lou to stop it straight away, but he didn't. Instead he started drumming along on the steering wheel, much to their delight. And with their encouragement, he acted up even more. The moshing as he drummed, I had to admit, was pretty funny, mainly because it was the uncoolest thing I'd ever seen, like watching your headmaster go on the pull, but when he started with the whole Britney Spears impression, it was just too much. For Maggie in particular, who cuffed him jokingly on the back of the head, telling him to concentrate on the road.

Things calmed down for a bit; the twins slumped into their seats, Mags seemed to be having a doze, while Ron had tuned into the dullest radio station I'd ever heard. Just endless loops of travel reports and news headlines. It was enough to make *my* eyelids droop, and I reckon had Ronnie not interrupted, I would have dropped off.

'Won't be long for you now, will it?' he murmured, eyes still on the road.

'Hhhhhm?'

'Until you can start driving. It's only two years away. You looking forward to it?'

'I suppose,' I answered, not wanting to sound too excited. After all, it wasn't as if I'd never driven before. Some of the kids I'd drunk with on the allotments had a habit of lifting motors and I'd joined them once or twice. They'd even let me drive one of the smaller ones round a car park. It wasn't too difficult as long as I didn't try to change gears. All that led to was kangaroo hopping, mostly into rows of shopping trolleys.

'You want to do the gears for a while? My lads always loved doing it.'

Course they did, I thought to myself, swallowing hard on the words.

'Why? Don't you know how to drive? You want to watch yourself, or they'll have you off the road.'

Ronnie just smiled and took his hand off the gear stick. 'Yeah, yeah, very funny. Come on. Quick! Fourth to third before that roundabout gets any closer.'

I joined in, more out of boredom than anything else, and it was a good way of messing with him a little bit, jumping down two gears at a time, making him lurch forward into the steering wheel. But to his credit he took it in good spirit and let me carry on, all the way to the campsite.

The site was actually pretty cool. All the pitches were tucked away in a wood, in their own little clearing, and each had its own fire pit.

The twins were beside themselves after the journey and ran into the forest in search of adventure. I expected Ronnie to yank them back until the tents were set up, but instead he watched them disappear with a smile on his face.

'Right then, Bill. Fancy helping me get started?'

Before I could answer, he bundled a load of sleeping bags into my arms and pointed me in the direction of the nearest path.

'Quick as you can. There's plenty more to carry before we can even begin putting the tents up.'

I didn't mind. It felt good to be away from home and out of Annie's grasp, so I kept my head down and watched the Ronnie and Maggie show.

They were like two scrapping rhinos. Both had big

personalities and even bigger gobs, and were quite happy to let the other know exactly what they were thinking.

'Why on earth are you putting that there?'

'Because it's in the shade under the tree, so the tent won't get hot in the morning.'

'Maybe not, but if it's windy you won't be able to sleep for the branches scraping against the sides.'

'Don't be so ridiculous. It's hardly going to keep me awake, is it?'

'All right. I have done this before, you know, but if you want to ignore me that's up to you.'

To anyone looking on, you'd think they'd been married years, not thrown together because they had no choice.

I stopped sorting out our tent to watch them every now and again, but eventually got right into putting our den together. I don't know where Ron had got the tents from, but ours was decent enough. It was a big old dome thing, high enough to just about stand up in, and it had loads of room inside. Once I'd rolled out the mats, sleeping bags and pillows, it looked properly comfy in there. I knew the twins would go mad for it.

By the time I'd finished, Ron was giving Mags a hand with her tent, rubbing it in that he'd finished before her. I took that as my cue to make an exit. If she stabbed him with a dirty tent peg, I'd probably end up taking the rap, knowing my luck.

It didn't take long to hunt the twins down. You could hear them a mile off, their whoops cutting through the trees. I found them by a river, the sort of place you usually see only in films. It divided the wood from a large field and the last of the trees hung over the water. Someone had obviously seen what a cool spot it was and had hung a rope from one of the highest branches, fastening an old tractor tyre to the end of it. Louie was heaving Lizzie over the water below and she was loving it, beaming from ear to ear as she edged closer and closer to the sky.

It filled me up to see them like that, not having to share the swing with eight other lifers, waiting as the scummers persuaded each one to take their turn.

For a second I got a glimpse of what a normal childhood might be like, and hoped that it would not be too late for them.

We spent the next hour catapulting each other across the river, and nothing could burst the bubble. Even when Louie tumbled out of the tyre and into the cold water below, the shock wasn't enough to put an end to the games. Instead, Lizzie jumped in too, kicking wave after wave on top of him, which led to the mother of all water fights.

Soaked to the skin and out of breath, we collapsed on to the bank, giggling at the mess we'd got ourselves into.

'Ronnie's going to do his nut when he sees us,' Lizzie said, laughing.

'I reckon we should fetch him down here and get him in the tyre as well. See if we can shake him into the river. Do you reckon we could, Bill?'

'After what I just saw, I reckon you could do it easy, Lou.'

Their imaginations went wild then as they came up with ways of getting even with Ronnie. It started with putting nettles in his socks and wild mushrooms in his breakfast, and ended up with shoving a nest of vampire ants into his sleeping bag, each idea being greeted with delight.

On our way back to the camp, though, Lou asked a question that I hadn't expected.

'Will we still be able to see Ronnie once we've gone to live at Mum's?'

I had no idea what to say, so I said nothing.

'Will we, Bill?'

'I reckon so. Maybe he'll be there when we see each other at weekends and that.'

'That's true. He used to drop us off at Jan's house when you were living there, didn't he?'

I shuddered at the memory.

'He used to buy us shed-loads of chocolate on the way home as well,' said Lizzie. 'Do you remember Lou?'

'Course I do. You used to cry like a baby until he agreed to stop and buy you some.'

'No, I didn't. Anyway, you were blubbing as much as me.'

'Cut it out. Both of you. It doesn't matter, does it?'

'Anyway, Louie,' Lizzie said in a told-you-so voice, 'Ronnie didn't mind. Just like he didn't mind sitting outside our room.'

'What do you mean?' I asked, my interest pricked.

'When you weren't there,' said Lizzie. 'He used to sit in the doorway, like you do. After reading your favourite stories and tucking the duvet under our feet.'

'He didn't need telling either,' added Louie. 'He knew what to do. And sometimes he sat there all night.'

'Don't be soft.' I could feel the frown snaking across my face.

'He did, though, Bill. There was one night when I woke up and really needed the loo, and when I came out he was still there. He had all these files and bits of paper around him, but he was still awake.'

'Did you ask him what he was doing there, Lou?'

'Why would I do that? He was just doing what you did. He was looking after us.'

And with that, we wandered along the path, towards a fire that smoked gently beside our tents.

CHAPTER 24

There was a lot to like about camping.

The lack of other lifers tearing around, getting in our faces. And no floors for Ronnie to mop, flooding the house with the smell of antiseptic.

But the thing I loved most about it was the abandoning of normal house rules.

First five p.m. came and went without a sniff of dinner, then eight without the briefest mention of bathtime, even from the Colonel. It felt like heaven, although I could see the twins trying to come to terms with the freedom.

'Don't we need to get into our bed things yet?' Louie had asked after clocking the time.

'No need for that tonight, Lou,' Maggie had replied. 'We're on camping rules tonight. The only rule is that we have no rules.'

I smiled as Lizzie turned her head to Ronnie, checking he wasn't going to overrule Mags, but he just nodded along as he laid sausages on a grill hanging above the open fire.

Maggie had pulled a blinder on the food front. We had burgers, sausages, kebabs, and spuds cooked in the fire, but when she passed us each an orange and told us we were going to make chocolate muffins from them, we thought she was off her tree.

Man, they tasted good. After we'd scooped out the insides and filled the shells with muffin mix, we wrapped them in foil and shoved them into the flames. For once, it wasn't the twins who were most excited. It was me. I couldn't stop myself from prodding at the orange, checking if the mix had set. In the end, Louie had to tell me to chill out, which drew hoots of laughter from the scum.

It didn't take long to get the muffin down me, and I had to bite my lip hard when Mags offered me hers as well. It seemed fair to let her have it. After all, it was her brain-wave.

So we sat and finished our food, or at least the others did, as the conversation drifted to other holidays we'd had as a house. Not a single one of them had been any good, but we were all so high on the chocolate that it didn't matter. All of a sudden, they were trips of a lifetime.

'Do you remember when we went to that hotel near the beach?' Louie beamed. 'And Tommy Saunders nicked the key to the cleaner's store cupboard?'

'I can hardly forget it, can I?' groaned Ron, as he forced down a smile. 'I was the one who found all the complimentary biscuits in his case.'

Maggie laughed so hard I thought she might choke. 'You have to give that boy credit. He might have been a thief, but at least he only nicked the bourbons. The jammy rings in my room were rubbish.'

'You may well laugh, Mags, but you weren't the one who had to drive him back there and explain what had gone on.'

'It was hardly worth the trip, though, was it? It was a few biscuits, not gold bullion.'

'Maggie! He'd dumped half of his clothes in the bin so he could fit more packets in his case. I could hardly let him get away with it, could I?'

With that, the three of us lost it. We remembered how excited Tommy had been to lift the key from the cleaner's cart and how many packets of biscuits we'd got through in our hotel rooms before Ronnie rumbled him back home. So many that we'd had to dump the wrappers in bins right along the beach, so the cleaner didn't catch on.

He may not have been a lifer for long, but Tommy reached legend status with that one.

By the time we'd exhausted the stories, the sun had disappeared and the fire had taken over as our light. I could see that both of the twins were tired, but I wasn't going to rush them into bed if the Colonel wasn't either.

In the end, Louie started to nod off in his chair, much to Lizzie's amusement.

Ronnie, not wanting to see the night ruined by him falling into the fire, bundled Louie over his shoulder and carried him into the tent.

Without being asked, Lizzie followed behind him, but not before asking me, 'Are you coming to bed as well, Bill?'

I screwed up my nose and shook my head. 'Nah. Reckon I'll sit here for a while. See if I can boss Mags into making me another muffin.'

Lizzie looked at me a second longer, long enough to convince me that she was going to ask me to sit in the door of the tent until she slept. But instead she just shrugged and smiled.

'Don't expect there to be any room on the mats, then,' she said, and giggled. 'Me and Lou reckon that tent's perfect for two, not three!'

Without a further word, she ducked inside.

I should've been pleased that they were happy to settle themselves that night. But her last words got under my skin. It looked like everything going forward was perfect for two, leaving me on my tod. Ronnie didn't help either when he came out of the tent. He wanted to talk more about the good old days, and that moment had passed. All I wanted to do was sit and stare into the fire.

'Funny, isn't it? Remembering all those holidays we had. What about that Outward Bound trip when we got stuck in that lodge in the snow. You were panicking we were all going to freeze to death. Or starve.'

'Hilarious,' I deadpanned, my eyes not leaving the flames.

'Reckon my favourite was that holiday park in Cornwall, though. They had the fastest water slides I'd ever seen.'

I didn't even bother responding.

Out of the corner of my eye, I saw him flick a look to Mags, who decided it was time to do the washing-up. Once she'd gone, he shuffled his chair closer to mine.

'You all right, Bill? You're very quiet all of a sudden.'

As he asked, he rested his hand on my shoulder, which tipped me over the edge. I shrugged him off as if he was diseased, frustration ripping through me.

'What is it with you? Why are you always so interested in how I'm feeling?'

'Whoa down, will you? I thought we'd had a good day. What's got into you all of a sudden?'

'Same thing as always. You. You never know when to leave alone, do you? You're always digging. Always trying to get inside my head.'

'I'm just trying to look out for you, aren't I? That's what I'm here to do.'

'No, that's what you're paid to do. And that sums it up, doesn't it, Ronnie? That's what I am. I'm not important to you really, am I? I'm just how you earn your money.'

'Bill, come on. You don't believe that, do you? Trust me, this isn't about money.' He tried to flash a smile at me. 'If you saw my wage slip, you'd know this isn't about money at all. I want to do what's right for you. Be someone you can trust. We've known each other such a long time now. I mean, we practically *are* family, aren't we?'

I was on my feet in a flash.

'Don't say that,' I spat. 'Don't you dare use that word. Not about me. Not about us.'

He looked confused. 'What word?'

'You know what word. *Family*. You've got *your* family. Your *wife*. Your precious *boys*. We see you, counting down the minutes to the end of your shift so you can run off home to them.'

'Come on, Bill. It's not like that. Believe me, it isn't. I think the world of you. I've known you longer than any of the other kids.'

'But I'll never be your son, so get that straight in your head, will you? I could never match up to your real boys, so don't even think about it. We all know the sun shines out of their arses.'

I saw a flash of irritation in his eyes as he leaned forward.

'Well, that just shows how much you really know, doesn't it?' He paused and fixed me with his best sergeant-major stare. 'Do you know the last time I saw my oldest lad?'

'Surprise me.'

'Six months ago.'

I rolled my eyes in disbelief, which he didn't take kindly to.

'Don't you look at me like that. Don't you dare sit there and suggest that I'm lying to you. I haven't seen him in six months, and then he only came round to tap me up for money.'

'What's his problem? You been trying to run his life like you do mine?'

'It's none of your business what the problem is.'

From the look in his eyes, though, I knew I wasn't far away from the truth.

'And that just makes my point for me, doesn't it, Ron? You know everything there is about me and I know nothing about you.'

'What do you mean?'

'All those files back home in the office. All those reports. All written by you. All the stuff about Shaun and what he did, you know it off by heart by now. But me, I don't even know where you live!'

He exhaled loudly and ran his fingers through his hair.

'Well, do you want me to tell you?'

'I don't give a shit where you live.'

With that he leapt out of his chair and paced to the other side of the fire. I could see that I'd got to him in a way that I never had before.

'Do you have any idea how frustrating it is trying to do right by you, Billy Finn? Every day I come into work, hoping I might see a flash of a smile from you, or even get a "good morning" past your lips. And more often than not I don't. Mostly I get to restrain you, which is the most hideous thing you could ask me to do.'

'Then don't do it. Can't say I enjoy it either.'

'What do you want from me, Billy?' He was really angry now, and as the flames snapped between us, it made him look almost demonic. 'What do you want to know? I tell you that I care about you and you sneer at me. I tell you that I don't even have a relationship with one of my sons and you throw it back in my face. What one thing can I tell you that would prove to you that I'm not just here to line my pockets?'

The words were out there before I could stop them.

'Where did you get your scars from?'

He stopped pacing and the flames stopped dancing in front of him.

'What scars?'

'The scars on your back. I saw them when we were training.'

I could see that he didn't want to answer, that I was trying to take him somewhere he didn't want to go, although he tried hard to hide it.

'I had an accident in the army. Early on. Nothing exotic. Didn't happen in combat, if that's what you're wondering.'

'So what happened, then?' I wasn't going to let this one go, wanted to test him all the way, see just what I actually meant to him.

'There are some things, Billy, that are best left in the past. It's not a pleasant story, you know.'

'And me being beaten by my stepdad is? Tell you what, then, I'll leave this alone if you never mention Shaun again, cos some things are best left in the past, you know.'

There was a nervousness to him that I didn't recognize as he sank into the chair next to me. Maybe it was the fire highlighting every line on his face, but he looked properly edgy as he started to speak.

'Joining the army was a big deal to me. I've never understood why I wanted to do it. I just did, ever since being a kid. So when I joined up I was in pretty good shape. I'd had friends who'd gone in before me and found basic training difficult. They spent more time throwing up and pulling muscles than they did out on parade, so I spent the summer getting myself ready. Basic training was a breeze as a result. There were plenty of others who struggled. I've never seen so much sick in my life.'

He looked at me, seeing if I was bored enough for him to stop, but I just stifled a yawn, which seemed to shame him into carrying on.

'By the time I passed out and joined my regiment, I was pretty much the biggest guy in there. Not the strongest or the quickest, but I was arrogant, you know. I wasn't scared to mix it up with any of them, and I reckon that got me noticed, especially by some of the older lads. I had a few scrapes when I first arrived, got involved in a few fights, made myself a bit unpopular with the people who mattered.'

'Did one of them set about you, then?'

He rubbed at his forehead with his fingers.

'Not exactly, but they found a way of bringing me down a peg or two.'

'Well? What did they do?'

'A lot of regiments have initiation ceremonies. Sometimes it's pretty tame, like proving you can hold your drink, or dumping you in the woods at night with no clothes or kit.'

'Sounds like a hoot,' I droned, trying to wind him up further.

'They decided – well, half a dozen of them did – that they wanted to see just how tough I was. So one night, while I was sleeping, they jumped me, blindfolded me and tied me up, and dumped me in the back of a wagon.'

I felt my body straighten up in the chair as my heart rate doubled in seconds.

'At first I tried to calm myself down. Reassure myself they were going to dump me in the forest like they'd done with some of the other lads. But when we stopped, we weren't in a forest. We were on this gravel track in the middle of nowhere. Anyway, they chucked me out the back of the truck, told me to strip off, then tied my hands to the tow bar.'

'Were you scared?'

'What do you think? I was terrified. Part of me reckoned they were just trying to put the wind up me, but I also knew that I'd really hacked some of them off, and they weren't the most forgiving sorts, you know?'

'But they were just winding you up, right?'

'Nope. Once they'd fastened me on with about ten foot of slack on the rope, they put the truck in gear and started to drive. Not fast at first, just enough to get me running at three-quarter pace and sweating. But when they got bored of me keeping up, they just knocked it up a gear.'

'What did you do?'

Ronnie looked at me as if I was mental. 'What do you think I did? I ran faster, didn't I? Or tried to. But the road started to wind and after a couple of minutes I couldn't stay on my feet, so they dragged me along on my back instead.'

'They stopped, though, didn't they?'

'Oh yeah, they stopped. After a hundred metres or something. But it was enough to scrape my back up pretty badly. The medics were picking gravel out of it for a good few hours. When they found me anyway.'

'You mean they left you there?'

'Well, they were hardly going to pat me on the back and congratulate me, were they? In their eyes I'd overstepped the mark, belittled them. This was their way of reasserting themselves.'

I didn't know what to do with myself. Couldn't quite believe what I was hearing.

'But you kicked their arses for it, didn't you? You said you could mix it up with any of them.'

'I could, but not collectively. There were six of them. And besides, I knew I could hurt them more without laying a finger on them.'

'I don't understand. How could you possibly get your own back without knocking them out?'

'Because the army was all these lads knew. They didn't have any other skills they could live off and they loved being part of this pack. So I hurt them that way. I had them chucked out.'

I tried to suppress a gasp but couldn't. 'You mean you grassed them up?'

'Yep,' he said, without a shadow of regret in his voice. 'I know I was young and annoying. I would have thought I was a complete tosser if I was them. But they could have killed me, Bill. If they'd gone a few metres more, or if I'd hit my head, that could have been it. Are you trying to tell me that all they deserved was a slap?'

'Well, no. But grassing them up? I thought you army types stood together.'

'We do. And I never had to grass anyone up in the next twenty years. I had a few scraps in that time, though.'

He stood by the fire, and kicked a couple of logs further into the flames.

'That's the thing, I suppose. Sometimes it's easier to have a fight, but the more you have, the harder it is to do anything else. That answer your question?'

I nodded, lost in my head. There didn't seem to be anything else to say.

'Well, I reckon I should go and give Mags a hand. She'll crucify me if I leave all the washing-up to her. Don't let that fire go out, will you? I fancy a brew before turning in.'

And without a backwards glance he pushed through the trees, leaving me with a lot to think about.

CHAPTER 25

The weeks that followed passed beneath a dark cloud. Stuff like the filming and the camping had been fun, but once they were over they just served as a reminder that everything was about to change. Whichever way I looked at it, the twins were going, and if that was the case, what was left for me?

My review had demanded good behaviour in return for keeping the three of us together, but with that chance in bits, I didn't see the point in playing ball any more.

School was the first thing to suffer. I mean, I was learning nothing, and spending all day doing it.

Some days I'd struggle in, just to kill a bit of time with Daisy, but other days even that wasn't enough and I'd lie in bed, trying to work out the best place to put my new star. So far it had remained in the box in the drawer. If I stuck it up somewhere it'd soon be as dull and lifeless as the others. That's what this place did to you.

Course, Ronnie noticed my change in mood, and although he did his best to gee me up, there were only so many beatings his body could take.

He encouraged me to go to the gym on my own and get stuck into the bags, but that held no appeal. I wasn't interested in boxing as a sport, so without someone to aim at there seemed little point.

In all honesty, the sparring had started to create problems of its own. The sessions had been all right for working through some stuff, but Shaun's face loomed larger every time I pulled on the gloves. Worse still, I found it difficult to forget about him once the session was over. I spent weeks chewing it over in my head, trying to understand it all. It had been years since I'd laid eyes on him, and I knew that he and Annie had split ages ago. So why was he coming back to me now? Why couldn't I shake his face from my head, or think about anything else except beating him the way he'd beaten me.

I carried him with me every day, whether I was awake or asleep, and I could feel him unravelling me slowly from the inside out. The anger that I'd been holding in, with the help of the boxing, was beginning to spill out, leaving me no option but to slip into old routines. I was back to walking the streets again, potting windows, breaking into cars, anything I could find to shift the clouds. Not even a bottle of cheap vodka flushed them away – and, believe me, I'd tried.

To make matters worse, things were pretty bleak with Daisy too. We still hooked up, but she was often subdued. She'd spend a load of time just staring into space, like she did when we first met. It was weird, but she looked smaller as well, like she was shrinking into her dad's shirts. She walked slowly, and always with her arms crossed, like she was continually hugging herself.

It wasn't until something happened at school that I

worked out what was going on. She'd been walking like a zombie down the corridor, ignoring me as I shouted her name. I bolted along behind her, grabbing her arm to get her attention. It wasn't as if I was being rough or anything, but she went mental at me, completely schizo.

'Get off me, will you?' she wailed, pulling her arm away, her face full of pain. 'What do you think you're doing, stalking up behind me?'

'Chill out, will you? I thought we were going to bunk off next lesson, that's all.'

'Don't give you the right to start mauling me, though, does it? Jesus, Billy, you're so rough.'

She was cradling her arms in front of her, and as I looked I could see a smear of blood on one of her sleeves, like a pen leaking in an inside pocket.

'You all right, mate? Your arm's bleeding.'

'No, it's not. It's nothing.'

'Don't look like nothing to me. It's getting worse. Want me to get you a plaster or something? You can't walk around like that.'

'Look, I told you. It's nothing. I must have scratched it . . .'

'That's not a scratch. You should get someone to –'

'Just LEAVE it, will you, Billy? Who do you think you are? Don't try and help me when you know nothing about me.'

She pushed on down the corridor and out of sight.

It didn't take much to work out what was happening and, once I had, I kicked myself for not realizing sooner.

Daisy was a cutter.

I'd seen it a few times with other lifers. Can't admit to

understanding it, but I knew it went on. There was one girl who'd lived with us for a while. She'd been moved from home to home. Reckoned she'd had a dozen placements in three years. No one believed her, but you could see she was screwed up. Rumour was she'd been messed about badly by some uncle or something, and by the time she arrived at our place she'd been cutting herself every day for months. She didn't last long with us. Couple of months until the scummers realized they were well out of their depth. Maggie spent hours at a time in the office, cleaning the cuts or talking to her therapist. Not that it did any good. As soon as the bandages were on, she'd just go to the other arm and start again.

One of the older kids asked her one night why she did it.

'Because I can. It's not as if I get choices about anything else. So this is the way I stay in control.'

We'd all sat there and tried to work out what she was going on about. It didn't make sense. Why would she choose to do that to herself?

One of the others reckoned she was just repeating what her shrink had told her, but that didn't make sense either. I mean, how could you be in control and choose to cut yourself open?

I wanted to ask her to explain it again, but within days she'd gone. What was one more placement to a girl who'd already had a dozen?

Realizing Daisy was in the same boat terrified me. All I wanted to do was tell her that it was OK, that I understood, but in fact neither of those things was true.

I tried to bring it up the next time we sat on the bench together. It was one of those days when she was more like her old self, gobbing off about some film she'd hated, how all it preached was subservience, whatever that was.

There'd been no mention of what had gone on in the corridor, and when I tried to bring it up, it was clear that she didn't want to go over it again.

'How have you been, then? The last few days?'

'What do you mean?'

'You know. I was just wondering how your arms were.'

Silence, except for the exhaling of cigarette smoke.

'I'm not trying to be nosy or anything, but –'

'Then don't ask me.'

'Come on, Daisy. I'm just trying to help, you know.'

'Well, there's no need. I'm dealing with it.'

'Didn't look like that the other day. It looked like you were in pain.'

'Look, Bill. I know you're trying to help. But you can't, all right. There are some things that talking about don't help. Most of the time I can deal with it, but not at the moment.'

'Why? What's happening?'

'Nothing's happening. It's just a difficult time of year, that's all. And no matter how much talking I do, that won't change. So why bother banging on about it?'

And that, it seemed, was that, as she picked tobacco off her tongue and stared off into the distance.

It was so frustrating. I thought we were getting beyond all the secrecy, that it was just easy between us. It's not like I was trying get in her pants or anything. Since her comment to the twins, I hadn't really thought about taking things further. No wonder when she was being so distant.

I worried about her, whether something had happened between her and the people she was living with. It was pretty obvious from the bits she'd said that they weren't close, but I wondered if something else was going on, that maybe they'd taken to knocking her about. I even thought about following her home, checking the place out, trying to get a feel for what was going on.

I didn't, of course. The risk of getting caught wasn't worth it, so instead I'd sit on our bench and watch her walk to the end of the road and out of sight, hoping the next day would see her in a better mood. I always gave her five minutes or so, then I'd walk the same road, and head to Jan and Grant's, hoping that one night I'd find the hall light on as I had done months ago.

Given my state of mind, I suppose it wasn't a surprise that I found myself outside their house more often than not. I'd stand there, leaning against the lamp post, kicking myself that things were so royally screwed up. I'd had my chance to be part of something and I'd blown it. No matter how many times I tried to blame them, I knew the person at fault was me. I didn't deserve them and they deserved better.

I don't know what I expected to find as I wandered round the ghost estate. After all, it had been years since I'd stepped foot anywhere near it.

I wasn't sure why I found myself on it now either. I was depressed enough at being shut out of Jan and Grant's, so why was I intent on making myself feel worse? Suppose I reckoned I deserved it.

There were pockets of the estate that still looked dog rough. You could have built entire cars out of the junk that littered some of the front gardens. But these were just the odd house every now and again, most places had a bit of pride about them. Not a lot of money spent on them, obviously, but they were tidy, cared for.

As I turned on to Forbes Ave, I expected the memories to prick away at me, but there was nothing. This wasn't home. It was just a place I'd lived in another lifetime.

One thing I did remember was the state of the house, because it always mirrored Annie's state of mind: a mess. There had never been time for gardening or DIY. Not when there was booze to be sunk. The only time her and Shaun ever spent in the garden was when the sun was out and there was enough benefit left to stretch to an eight-pack of lager or, if they were feeling flush, a bottle of cheap whisky. Anyone digging up the yard in a hundred years' time would think they'd found an ancient brewery or something.

I suppose I was here to do some digging of my own, desperate to find the house in the same crappy state. To find one thing I could take back to Ronnie, something that would make him say, 'You're right, Bill. She's no good for the twins. Let's call the whole thing off.'

But as I stood and stared at Annie's place, I felt all hope dissolve, because it looked normal. There were no beer cans in the yard, no empty bottles of wine stood on the windowsills, just an average, small, terraced house. It annoyed me so much that I bent down and picked up a lump of earth and readied myself to hurl it at the window. But before I could swing my arm I heard a voice behind me.

'Billy?' said Annie, squinting into the darkness. 'What the hell are you doing here?'

The mud fell to the ground as I struggled to find an answer, and when nothing sprang to mind, she cut back in.

'Are you all right? You look a bit pale.'

Like she cared.

I blurted out, 'No, I'm fine. Don't know why I'm here really. I'll be off . . .' and I walked past her.

'Was there something you wanted to talk about?' she shouted, which stopped me in my tracks.

There was loads I wanted to say to her, but I doubted she wanted to hear any of it. So instead I gave her the simple truth.

'You want to know why I'm here? I wanted to check your house out, because the last time I saw it, it wasn't fit for living in. It was a shit-hole.'

She didn't react in the way I'd expected her to. In fact, she barely reacted at all. She just wore the same expression, a mixture of confusion and sadness.

'Well, why don't you come and take a look, then? Be a shame to come all this way and not check it out. The windows definitely look better if they're not broken, I know that much.'

I'd hoped she hadn't noticed the mud I'd been holding, but I wasn't going to apologize for it. A broken window was the least she deserved.

'I don't want to set foot in that place. Coat of paint won't change what went on in there.'

As the words reached her, I saw the cracks begin to show. Her hand delved into her bag and whipped out her fags. I could see her shake slightly as she put fire to one, and she sucked in deeply like she was pulling on an inhaler.

'That was a long time ago, Bill. Things change, you know?'

'Do they?' I spat. 'I don't think they do. You might be able to convince the others, the social workers and counsellor scummers. But not me. I know what you're about.'

'Really? And what's that, then?'

'Same as you always were. You're a drunk and you're a liar.'

She rubbed her forehead with her hand, the smoke from her cigarette swirling round her head like a dirty halo.

'I'm an alcoholic, Bill, that bit's right. But I haven't had a drink for over three years now. I can tell you the date if you like.'

'Yeah, why don't you do that? Shame you can't remember the date of your own kids' birthdays, though, isn't it?'

'I know when you were all born. As if I'd forget that.'

'Then why don't you manage to get cards in the post? Lose our address or something?'

Her head hung low as she lit a second cigarette with the end of the first.

'You're stuck in the past, Bill. I haven't forgotten the twins' birthday in years.'

'Mine's a different matter, though, isn't it?' I spat, but once the words were out there, I instantly regretted them.

'Look, Bill, let's not do this out here. Come in and have a cup of tea with me.'

She tried to guide me down the path.

The hairs on my arms stood up at her touch. These weren't a mother's hands. They weren't gentle or soft, they weren't the hands that had calmed me after a bad dream or rubbed me better when I fell over. Her hands were rough, older than she was. They were a stranger's hands.

'I don't think so, Annie.' And I saw her flinch as I used her name. 'I didn't come here to make conversation. I just had to see the house. For the twins, not for me. I'll never step foot inside, not after what you let him do to us in there.'

I made to walk away, but she had other ideas.

'You think I can forget what happened either, Billy? I've been stuck in that house on my own for years, with nothing *but* memories about what he did to you. What I let him do.'

The tears welled in her eyes, but they were cold tears. They held no regret for me, just for herself.

'But I'm a different person now. I'm sober. And I want to make things better. I can't make it all right, I know that, but I can try and make it better.'

'What, by splitting us up? By taking away the only person that's always been there for them? You're just worried I'll tell them the truth about you. About what a drunk you are. About how you sat there and watched your boyfriend beat me, just because I wasn't his!'

A light went on in my head.

'That's why you signed those papers, isn't it? That's why you wanted me to go to Jan and Grant's? Cos Shaun didn't want me. And with me out of the way, the twins might remember you as something you never were – a decent mother.'

The tears rolled down her cheeks and she made no attempt to wipe them away.

'You can't think that, Bill. I didn't realize what I was doing. I was still drinking, still drunk. They told me I'd never get you back, that it was kinder to let you have a second chance with someone else.'

'Who told you that?' I yelled. 'Shaun? You listened to him?'

'No, it wasn't him. It was the social workers. They told me I wasn't capable of looking after you. That you had needs that other people might be able to handle. Things I wouldn't be able to cope with.'

'So you gave up on me, just like that?'

'That's not how it was, Billy. But you were so angry. I didn't know what to do with it. How to make it any better. You were so . . . so . . . angry!'

I tried to swallow the bile in my throat, determined to show her that I could do calm, but the anger was burning, and unless it came out I thought I'd explode.

'And whose fault is that, Annie? Who's to blame there? Let's think, shall we? Who did I learn that one off?'

'I was never angry with you, Billy. I was just ill. I didn't know what I was doing.'

'But you stood there and you watched him. You watched Shaun as he took me apart. And you never stopped him. Not once.'

'I wanted to, though. I did. I was just scared.'

'You weren't scared, Annie,' I said, shaking my head slowly. 'You were just pissed. It was easier to be pissed than be a mum, and that's why you stayed with him. Because he gave you what you needed. He gave you booze.'

I started to walk on. I'd heard all I wanted to hear, but that didn't stop her, and she practically ran after me, shouting manically as she went.

'But I'm sober now, Billy. Do you hear me? I've changed. But you,' she spat, 'you haven't. And you know what, that's why that family sent you back. Because you won't let anyone near you, let alone love you.'

'And whose fault is that?' I asked her.

I walked on a few steps before stopping one last time to face her.

'I know the twins are coming to you, because I know you've convinced them all that you can do it. But just remember, I know you better, and when you mess up – WHEN, not if, WHEN – the twins will never forgive you, and neither will the scummers. Then we'll see who's unlovable, won't we?'

As the last of the words fell out of my mouth, I could see doubt take root in her head, but I took no pleasure from it. Whatever happened next meant pain for someone, whether it was the twins or me. And all I could do, it seemed, was wait for it to happen.

CHAPTER 26

For normal kids, bank holidays mean trips to the seaside, long days in the park or the chance to be spoilt rotten by grandparents. There's a separate set of rules for a lifer's bank holiday. In my world, the three-day break was seen as the perfect time to send the twins to live at Annie's.

It was the beginning of the end of the world. After today, their heads would be full of Annie and their new room, the friends they'd play with in their street. It would only be a matter of time – weeks, I reckoned – until they forgot about this place. Forgot about me.

Ronnie tried to put a gloss on it, promised to keep me busy with training, and loads of one-on-one time, but it was no use. There was nothing he could offer that would soften the blow or make me feel less alone.

I watched the light invade my room that morning, the same way I had for the past few months, dozing fitfully as Louie curled himself next to me. His visits had become a nightly event since he'd learned of their return to Annie's, and as much as I worried about how he would cope once there, I didn't have the heart to put him back in his own bed. Besides, his company meant I relaxed enough to grab patches of sleep as well.

Lizzie, on the other hand, seemed more at ease about it all, excited even, and only really joined Louie when she woke to realize he wasn't there.

They knew what was going on. The scummers had gone into overdrive to prepare them, constantly encouraging them to be as independent as possible. They even brought in this counsellor, who had them drawing pictures about what life would be like at their mum's. I don't know whose drawing killed me most. Lizzie's picture was so detailed. A house and garden, with her, Annie, Louie and me waving happily from the doorway, whereas Louie's was a one-colour scribble. There was no inviting smoke coming from his chimney, no garden in bloom, while the three figures he'd drawn certainly weren't smiling. And I was nowhere to be seen.

I think this must have freaked the scummers out a bit, as I got this lecture from the counsellor about the part I could play in preparing them. I was told to talk to them regularly, whenever I could or whenever they had questions. What did they expect me to say? How could I tell the twins it was for the best, when all I wanted to do was lock them in my room and never let them out of my sight? It stank. The whole thing stank, but I had no way of getting out of it.

As I slumped down the stairs on that final morning, I had no idea of how we were going to fill the hours before Annie's arrival. All I'd been told was that we had to make it as normal as we possibly could, for the sake of the twins. Fortunately, Ronnie had planned the morning with his normal military precision, and for once I just went with it. I didn't have the fight in me to disagree.

He'd started off with a full English, which broke his golden rule of fry-ups being only a Sunday treat. Watching him destroy his mountain of food, I wondered if this abandoning of barrack rules was just for his own pleasure.

He hadn't let us off the washing-up of course and it had taken us a good half-hour to get everything gleaming to his standards. As we finished the drying, I noticed that the other lifers were being gently prodded out of the door, and judging by the amount of stuff they were carrying, they wouldn't be back for the rest of the day.

I had to admit, it was a relief to see them go. The last thing I needed was someone getting in my face. I didn't want to spend my last morning with the twins eating carpet for giving someone what they deserved.

Ron seemed relieved to see them go too. As the minibus swung out of the gates, I saw his face relax slightly, although it still wore the creases of a worried man as he turned to face us.

'Right then, troops. Shall we have a sit in the lounge? Billy's got something that you might want to watch.'

I frowned as I tried to work out what he meant.

'The life-story book, Bill?' he whispered. 'I thought this would be a good time to show it to the twins. You want me to grab it from your room?'

'Er, no. It's fine. I'll get it,' I said.

Although I hadn't thought of watching it with them, I supposed it made sense. So I could explain what it was for, and so they could take it with them.

It was a bit weird watching it. I hadn't dared to look at it since Daisy had handed it over. But the twins seemed to get what it was about, once they'd stopped howling with laughter at me talking to the camera. They had both wanted to sit next to me, although once it was in full flow, Lizzie slid on to the floor and laid on her front, chin resting on her hands. You'd have thought she was watching *The Princess Bride* again, not her brother bumbling his way round the house.

Louie remained next to me, and while he giggled at the memories of the gallery wall, I could feel the tension in him, the firmness of his grip, as he pushed his hand into mine. I squeezed gently and pulled him close to me.

It wasn't until it was nearly finished, and Ronnie appeared on the screen, that I really paid attention. To be honest, I'd forgotten that he'd hijacked Daisy and the camera that day, and watched nervously as he began to speak.

'Hello, you two. It's me, Ronnie.'

Despite the casualness of his words, there was still an air of the military about him as he sat, ramrod straight, hair neatly combed.

'I hope you don't mind me butting in on Billy's film, but I just wanted to say hello and, er, goodbye as well. I've had the honour of being your key worker all this time. In fact, I was there on the very night that the three of you arrived. It seems hard to believe that you've been here ever since and that we've all been together so long. I just . . . well, I suppose I just wanted to tell you to enjoy life back at your mum's. It's a wonderful thing to have a family, and you only ever get one mum, so look after her, and behave for her as well.

I've lost track of how many times I've had to make your beds over the years, so don't have Annie running after you like I have, you hear?'

He waved as he finished his speech and the camera angle fell as Daisy began to lower her arm. But the camera never flicked off, as Ron butted back in.

'Oh, just one more thing. I'm sure Billy has done a brilliant job of showing you around the house you've lived in all this time. But if there's one thing that you must never forget in the years ahead, it isn't this house, or any of the carers that have looked after you.

'The thing you mustn't ever forget is your brother. Because Billy . . . well, I've never met anyone like your brother, and he's the reason you've grown up to be as brilliant as you are. Sometimes I forget that he's only six years older than you. I shouldn't. But I do. He's been like your mum and dad rolled into one for the last eight years. So, whatever you do, don't forget that. And don't forget to ring him as well. Go on now, go off and have some fun. I'll see you soon.'

With that, the screen fuzzed to black, before I heard my voice again coming from the screen. But I couldn't see for the tears that were stinging my eyes.

I don't do tears. Haven't done for years. Being angry generally gets in the way. So when I started misting over at Ron's words, I didn't know what to do except choke them down before anyone saw. I managed to get them down past my throat, where my anger usually sits, just before it explodes everywhere.

Once the DVD finished, the Colonel appeared at the door.

'Right then, you two, your mum's going to be here in an hour, so I need you to go upstairs and check every bit of your bedroom and make sure every last toy is packed and in your bags. I'm not running over to your house last thing tonight just because you've forgotten something.'

The twins rolled their eyes before ambling out of the room, probably wondering if that was the last time they'd have to listen to him having a moan.

'You all right, Bill?' he asked.

I didn't dare mention the film, his bit especially, not with the tears still swimming near the surface. Instead I just nodded.

'I know it's not going to be easy today. But I'm going to be here all weekend in case you want to talk.'

I frowned. 'What do you mean all weekend? Doesn't your shift finish tonight?'

'Should do. I just thought it might be better if I stuck around, you know . . .'

I could see the fear in his face. The fear that I'd give him the same brush-off that I always had. So when I just nodded and walked past him, he looked properly relieved.

The twins' room looked weird. With the beds stripped and the walls empty of their posters – well, except for half-peeled football stickers – it looked like a room in a crappy hostel. Which, I reckoned to myself, was just about what it was.

They'd scoured the room and crammed the remaining bits and pieces into their bags. It all looked so final now that I was desperate to get out of there and back downstairs.

'Come on, then,' I said, surprised by how chipper my

voice sounded. 'Let's get your kit out of here. She'll be here soon.'

As much as I wanted to stop time in its tracks, I knew it couldn't happen. And in fact, it felt like only seconds later that Dawn (unbelievably, still our social worker after eight long months) rapped on the door, Annie lurking behind her.

'Hello, all,' Dawn chirped, her smile fading a little as her eyes landed on me.

Lizzie couldn't get past her quick enough and almost knocked Annie clean off her feet as she leapt into her arms.

'Hello, my love,' Annie sighed as she pushed her face into Lizzie's hair. 'I'm so pleased to see you. You're looking pretty today.'

'Are we going home now?' Lizzie asked, throwing looks at Dawn, Annie and Ronnie, like she was unsure of who was in charge any more.

'Soon, Lizzie, soon,' answered Annie, as she looked around. 'Now, where's your brother? I haven't even seen him yet.'

I frowned as I scanned in front of me, but she was right. No Louie. I looked over my shoulder to find him stood right behind me, a frown threatening to take over his face.

'What are you doing there, Lou?' Ronnie asked quietly. 'Aren't you going to say hiya to your mum?'

'Hiya.' He waved, an attempt at a smile on his lips. But he didn't move from behind me.

'Right,' said Dawn, breaking the tension quickly. 'Why don't I start loading up the car and leave you to say your goodbyes?'

She grabbed an armful of kit and hoisted it over her shoulder, before scuttling away as quickly as she could.

'Louie?' came Annie's voice. 'Louie, I know this is bound to feel weird today. But it's going to be OK, I promise. It feels weird for me too. I've been waiting for this for a long time. But I promise you, it's going to be fine. More than fine. It's going to be great.'

She held out her hands to him and slowly he edged closer to her, before allowing her to fold him into her arms.

He stayed there for a second or two, then levered himself backwards, his eyes flicking over to me, to see my reaction.

'Can Billy come with us, Mum?' he asked quickly, hope appearing suddenly in his voice. 'Just for an hour or two this afternoon?'

Annie didn't know what to say. She looked around, hoping Dawn was on her way back, ready to dive in and save her. Luckily for her, Ronnie did what he always did and butted in.

'I don't think that's a good idea today,' he said, stroking the top of Louie's head. 'Any other day, I'm sure that would be fine. But today it would be best if you went with just Dawn and your mum. Give yourself time to settle in at home. Get your stuff unpacked and your pictures on the wall. It'll be nicer for Billy to see it when it's finished, won't it?'

'Suppose,' Louie answered, his eyes still fixed on mine.

'And don't forget. We've arranged a visit for next Saturday afternoon. We're going to meet at Pickering Park, then go for a pizza. That's only seven days, mate.'

'It'll pass in no time,' said Annie, unmistakably relieved that Ronnie was there. 'Look, why don't I take the rest of the bags to the car and give you some time to say goodbye to Ronnie and Bill? I'll wait for you there.'

She picked up their two small bags, before sparing me a smile, the best one she had in her locker. 'Thank you so much, Billy. I don't know what else to say. Except, you know, I'm sorry.'

'What for?' I asked sharply. 'For what you said to me the other week?'

Ronnie's face creased in confusion, but he said nothing.

'For that and everything else.' For a second, I saw emotion in her eyes and hoped it was regret.

'I don't know what else to say to you, Billy. I wish I knew.'

Try *I've changed my mind*, I thought to myself. In fact I'd even settle for *Come with us*. Anything that meant they weren't going to walk through that gate with her today. Not without me.

As she left, I couldn't help but notice how small their bags actually were. That the contents of their lives could be shoved inside two simple holdalls. They deserved more than that. We all did.

I looked at Lizzie and smiled, before grabbing her under her arms and swinging her into a bear hug. Her breathing was short and sharp, the tears starting to interrupt the rise and fall of her chest.

'We both want you to come with us, Billy,' she cried. 'I don't understand why you're staying here. Don't you want to come?'

'It's not about what I want, matey,' I said gently. 'We've talked about this, haven't we? It's about getting you settled. I'd be leaving home in a couple of years anyway. It wouldn't be fair on Annie to make her move to a bigger house, only for me to then move out, would it?'

'You will be there next week, though, won't you?' she asked.

'Wouldn't miss it,' I replied, before forcing a grin on to my face. 'Especially as Ronnie's paying.'

She giggled loudly as she pressed into me for one last cuddle.

'Annie will sit outside the bathroom while I'm in there, won't she, Bill?' she whispered, embarrassed that Ronnie might hear.

'You won't need her to, mate, honest you won't. But all you have to do is ask her,' I replied, setting her down on the ground before my back broke.

All that left was Louie, growing paler by the second. I beckoned him over as I perched on the porch step. He sat sadly on my knee and let his head fall on to my chest.

'I'm not going,' he said firmly, and as he said it, I heard Ronnie take a step closer. I had to jump in quickly before he did it for me.

'Come on, mate. That doesn't make sense, does it? This is what we've talked about for years. A proper home, away from here. In fact, this is better than what we dreamed about. You're going to be with your mum!'

'How can it be better, Billy, if you're not there?' he asked. 'That wasn't what we talked about.'

'But it doesn't change anything, Lou. It's just geography. So what if I'm not sleeping there? All you have to do is pick up the phone and I'll be there, you know that.'

'But I haven't got a phone, have I?' he cried seriously.

'No, you muppet. But Annie does. You just use hers.'

'Don't make me go, Bill. I don't want to.'

'That's not true, though, is it? You're just feeling like this because you're leaving. In an hour or two you'll feel different.'

'But if I don't, will you come and get me?'

I looked him squarely in the face. 'If you need me, really need me, and if Annie can't make whatever it is better, all you have to do is call me. I won't turn my phone off, I promise.'

That seemed to be enough and he pushed himself into me, filling my chest, my entire body, with warmth. I tried to store it up, wring every last ounce of emotion out of it that I could, scared shitless that it would be a long time until I felt anything like it again.

Before I knew it, Lizzie was there too, burrowing her way into me, which pushed the tears from my throat into my mouth. As much as I wanted them to stay, I knew I could only hold the tears in so long. And all I could do was think to myself, *Please don't cry. Please don't cry.*

The tears were pricking my eyes when I heard the Colonel come to my rescue.

'Come on now, you two. Let your brother breathe. It really is time to go.'

With that I felt them slide away from me, and with every step they took, I felt something rip wider and wider apart, the feeling so intense that it took everything I had to stop shouting out in pain.

By the time they walked slowly up the path I could barely think straight. My hand was waving automatically, but everything else was just focused on keeping it all together.

It was only when the gate slammed shut and they disappeared from sight that the tears really came. And it was then that I turned to Ronnie and without thinking, and without worrying or caring, wrapped my arms around him and allowed him to hold me up.

CHAPTER 27

The mug of tea sat stewing in my hand. It had been piping-hot twenty minutes before, threatening to warm up my shivering body, but now it was just lukewarm and half-empty.

Ronnie perched on the bench next to me, draining the dregs of his cup, before sighing loudly.

'How's that going down?'

'It's not, really.'

'I know what you mean. I'd rather it was a pint,' he said, staring off into the distance.

'Tell me about it.'

He laughed quickly through his nose. 'Eighteenth birth-day, Billy. There's a table in the local, right in front of the fire, reserved for me and you.'

I didn't think I could wait three years for a single pint. Waiting a couple of hours to down a bottle of . . . well, whatever I could find seemed like a stretch at the moment.

'How are you feeling? You look cold.'

I didn't know how to answer, as I didn't feel anything. Except numb.

I had no idea how long had passed since the gate had

slammed closed, only that my eyes were sore, that my mind was tired and that I had no tears left.

'I'm sorry,' I said, without looking up.

'What are you sorry for?'

'You know, for breaking up like that. I didn't mean for you to have to deal with it.'

'Don't be ridiculous.' He sighed, bumping his shoulder with mine. 'That's what it's all about. I'd have been more worried if you hadn't drenched me, to be honest. And I'd rather you cried than try to lay me out.'

A snort of laughter came out of my nose, but I sniffed it straight back, guilty that I could find anything to smile about.

'It'll get easier, you know.'

'What will?'

'Them not being here. It won't feel easy for a while, but I promise you, Bill, it will get easier in time.'

I exhaled slowly, not knowing what to say. I wanted to believe him, trust that what he said was true, but I just couldn't see it.

'It doesn't matter.' I sighed. 'Don't worry about it. I'm sure it won't be your problem for long anyway.'

Ronnie shifted his weight forward on the bench as the words reached him.

'What do you mean? Of course it's my problem. You've been my problem all this time. Why should anything change now?'

'Because I won't be here long, will I?'

'What gave you that impression? This is your home, Billy. Just because the twins have gone, that won't change.'

I sighed again and rubbed at my stinging eyes, all emotion drained from my voice.

'And what about what they said at my review? About me getting too big for this place. About moving me on to that therapeutic unit or whatever they called it.'

'Billy, they talked about that place because they were worried about you. Worried that you were going to end up hurting someone, or, more importantly, hurting yourself. But I've seen you, Bill, I've seen you change so much over the last few months, and I'm not talking about turning up at school, or any of that rubbish. I'm talking about how you were with the twins, with the other kids here. With Daisy. With me.'

'I haven't changed. I was just acting. Putting it on so you'd let them stay with me.'

'I don't believe you. I know you've been trying, that's been obvious to everyone here. But don't you sit there and tell me that you haven't felt different lately. That it hasn't felt like an improvement to how things were. Because that's rubbish, Billy, and you know it.'

I sat and looked him in the eye, amazed. Amazed that he'd called me a liar to start with, but even more amazed that he had this opinion of me. That he'd been watching me to that extent.

'What does it matter anyway?' I bluffed. 'Whatever I've thought these last few months, none of that means anything any more, does it? The twins have gone. Annie's got her own way. Who gives a shit what happens to me now?'

'Well, I do, Billy,' he yelled, rising from the bench. 'Don't you realize that? I've been here for you ever since you arrived, my friend. Now, that may mean nothing to you, but it means a lot to me. So don't expect me to stick around and watch you mess everything up.'

'Do what the rest of the scummers do, then. If you don't like it, if we're too much for you to handle, then fuck off and do something else.'

I paused as I watched him sit back down, his air of invincibility punctured.

'Oh aye, and what else would I do?'

'I don't know. Go back to the army? I don't care.'

'I'm too old for that.' He chuckled, although it wasn't a laugh filled with joy. 'I'm too old and too stuck in my ways for much, to be honest.' He looked me in the eye. 'I did think about leaving once. Was on the verge of handing in my notice, had the letter written and everything. Scared me rigid, it did. I had no idea what I was going to do or what I had to offer. When you've been here as long as I have, you wonder if you could ever fit in anywhere else.'

The recognition of what he said took the wind clean out of me.

'So what happened?' I asked.

'What do you mean?'

'Why did you change your mind?'

'We had a phone call, didn't we? Late at night. I was going to hand in my letter the next morning as my shift ended. But the phone call made me change my mind.'

'Why? What was it about?'

'It was about you, Bill. Your placement with Jan and Grant had broken down and you were coming back. I couldn't exactly quit then, could I?'

He pushed his arm around me and rested his hand on my shoulder.

'I'm glad I didn't as well. Despite the chunks you've taken out of me over the years. Because no matter what you think of me, or of yourself, I know it was worth it.'

I was speechless. I mean, what do you say to that?

Nothing.

Except fight back the new wave of tears that had gathered inside.

We spent the afternoon mooching about. Ronnie tried to get me in the gym, but I wasn't interested. So instead we went wandering. Nowhere in particular, just walking. It wasn't as if we spent the whole time talking either. My brain was too busy trying to take in what he had told me, about leaving, about staying, about what he thought of me.

As hard as I tried, I couldn't make sense of it. It just didn't add up, that he'd stay because of me. Why would he do that? Why would he do that *for me*?

My head kept fixing on what he'd said, about not being able to move on, not being able to fit in anywhere else. It shocked me, I suppose, that this bloke, who always looked in such control, could possibly feel the same way I felt.

Part of me reckoned he was spinning a line to make me feel better, but part of me didn't. There was an honesty to what he'd said and the way he'd said it. A sadness, I suppose, a recognition that he was stuck, going nowhere.

As we approached home, I felt my body sag, the emotion of the day and the constant whirring of my head finally taking its toll. It was only eight o'clock, but I was done. I wanted nothing but bed and my faded stars.

'Why don't you head off, Ronnie?' I said to him as we traipsed through the front door. 'Seriously, I'm just going to crash. You don't need to stay, honest.'

'I know I don't need to stay, but I'm going to anyway. And before you say anything, I know you don't need baby-sitting, so get yourself upstairs and in bed before I try to read you a story.'

I spent the next couple of hours drifting in and out of sleep, dozing and dreaming, being visited by everyone and anyone: the twins, Ronnie, Annie, social workers of Christmas past, they came and went, telling me to relax, that everything was going to be fine. And I was cool with that, until Shaun started whispering the same words into my ear: *It's OK, it's OK, Daddy's here . . .*

With that, I was bolt upright, the green glow of my phone cutting through the darkness.

'1 new message' it read, and for a second I dared not open it, something in my head telling me it was going to be Shaun whispering more sweet nothings to me.

Shaking my head to dislodge the idea, I picked up the phone, hoping it would be from the twins, though I couldn't work out what I wanted it to say.

As the message opened I was left looking at Daisy's name and a text that offered hope for tomorrow:

```
hpe u r ok. Bin thnkng bout u. minesweepng
2mrow?
```

I flopped back on to the bed, my fingers tapping out the briefest reply:

```
Perfect
```

I let the phone fall on to my chest and breathed deeply, hoping that Daisy might offer some answers to the questions in my cluttered head.

All I had to do now was sit, count and wait for the morning.

CHAPTER 28

There's nothing worse than waking up with a hangover. Especially when you haven't even been drinking. I was up predictably early, well before the rest of the house, so I dragged my duvet down to the TV room and sat in front of the box.

I'd searched at first for the copy of *The Princess Bride* that Daisy had lent us, but I couldn't find it anywhere. One of the lifers must have snaffled it, so I made a mental note to hurt someone over it later and settled instead for some channel-hopping. Of course nothing was hitting the spot. The kids' programmes niggled at my pounding head and the music channels were pumping out nothing but pop, so I settled for the replay of yesterday's football.

It did the job, I suppose, gave me something to at least try and concentrate on. But it didn't matter how many screamers flew in, or how many times someone dived, nothing lifted my mood for even a second.

Perhaps it was the tiredness and the build-up of sleepless weeks that was doing it, but I couldn't quieten what was going on in my head.

I was gutted, angry and confused. I didn't know who to

believe or what the future meant, and all that my mind could do was spin around on one gigantic loop, throwing each question up in turn. As the questions repeated, they got louder, and faster, until I honestly thought the top of my head was going to come off. So after chucking on some clothes and grabbing my phone, I headed out, being careful not to wake Ronnie or the other scummers as I left.

I started in the gym, wondering if half an hour on the heavy bag might kick-start my day and quieten my mind, but as hard as I tried, I just couldn't build any enthusiasm for it, and to be honest I didn't fancy inviting Shaun into my pounding head.

I stuck around in the garage for a while, though, tidying the equipment and sweeping the floor, doing anything that might settle me down, but nothing seemed to work. So I took to the streets and headed for the bench, knowing it wouldn't be long until Daisy surfaced.

On the way, I stopped at Jan and Grant's, and my heart raced as I saw the car missing from the drive. I couldn't think of a reason for them being out so early on a Sunday and my mood lifted at the chance of them being away for the bank holiday. I toyed with the idea of taking a closer look, but the street was starting to wake up, and with the first of the Sunday morning car-washers appearing in the driveways, I decided against it and wandered on, knowing I'd be back later.

It felt good to be perched on the bench, a relief more than anything to be out of home, and it didn't take Daisy long to reply to the text I'd bashed out when I arrived.

Within half an hour, she was ambling towards me, fag in

hand as per usual, but more importantly in a decent mood. In fact, she greeted me with a hug, which I didn't quite know what to do with, so I just hung on for as long as she did, putting my arms in the same place as hers.

'So,' she said, sighing, 'how did it go?'

I exhaled loudly, not knowing what to say.

'That well, eh?'

'Oh, mate, I don't know where to start. It was the hardest thing I've ever done. I had to stand there and practically talk them into going with her. Louie was petrified. They must have thought I *wanted* rid of them or something.'

'Don't be ridiculous. They know how you feel. And anyway, what else could you do? Whether you talked them into it or not, they were leaving. What was the alternative? Ronnie carrying them to the car kicking and screaming?'

'Doesn't make it any easier, though, you know? My head feels mashed. I haven't got a clue what's going to happen now.'

I spent the next fifteen minutes talking about the previous day, and Daisy sat quietly, listening and smoking.

'What did I tell you about that Ronnie?' she said, jabbing me in the ribs with her lighter. 'I told you he was a dark horse, didn't I? You've sat there, night after night, slagging him off, and it turns out you're the reason he stayed. You've got to listen to that, Bill. That guy cares for you and that has to mean something, doesn't it?'

'The thing that surprised me most, though, was the stuff he said about not being able to fit in anywhere else. I didn't have a clue that he could feel like that. I mean, he's the Colonel!'

'Doesn't mean he can't feel things, does it? You haven't got the monopoly on feeling screwed up, you know?'

'I know that,' I huffed, 'but as soon as he said it, I wanted to shout, *That's how I felt!*'

'What do you mean?'

'You know, when the whole adoption thing broke down. No matter how hard I tried to blame everyone else, the truth was, it was *my* fault. I just couldn't fit in. It was just, I don't know, too different.'

'In what way?'

'All I can remember, for the whole of my life, is living with loads of kids. At Oldfield, there's always been, like, ten of us. So when I arrived in the new house and there was just me and two adults, I don't know, I just couldn't get my head around it.'

'Did you tell them how you felt?'

'I couldn't, could I? They would have thought I was mental. And the truth was, they were doing their best. Everything they bought me was brand new. I had new clothes, a new computer, everything was mint out of the box, but I didn't know what to do with it all. It isn't what happens to kids like us, you know? We're used to hand-me-downs and second best.'

'But that's not your fault, Bill, to be confused by it all.'

'Yeah, but I didn't handle it well, did I? The harder they tried, the harder I pushed back. It was like I had to test their commitment, had to show them that I wasn't worth it. When they gave me choices about what I wanted to do or eat, I wouldn't answer, sometimes to test them, but sometimes because I just didn't know what to say. I'd gone from having no choices at all to too many, and sometimes my head couldn't keep up.'

'Is that why things broke down with them?'

I cringed at the thought. *If only it had been that simple.*

'Not exactly.'

'Then what was the problem?'

I chewed the inside of my cheek, knowing she was pushing me into dangerous territory.

'Come on, Bill, you can tell me. You know that.'

My body tensed at the suggestion.

'You don't want to know. Trust me.'

'I do trust you, you idiot. That's why I spend so much time with you. And let's face it, it's not because of your money, is it?'

I knew what she was trying to do, but raising a smile wasn't going to make it any easier and in the end, after another painful silence, she went on.

'Look, Bill. I know you've told me loads lately, and I really love that you've wanted to. I know as well that I haven't told you much, about me and that. But that's not because I don't trust you, it's just that stuff has happened to me in the past, stuff that I'm still trying to get my head around. What I'm trying to say is that, for a long time, I blamed myself completely for what happened to me. I couldn't accept that it could be anyone else's fault but mine. So I bottled it up and wouldn't talk about it, and that's when things got worse, believe me.'

'But I did something terrible, Daisy . . .'

'Listen, there's nothing you can say that would shock me. Believe me. For a long time I thought I was responsible for my mum and dad *dying*. Do you hear me, Billy? That it was my fault. And it wasn't until I took a risk and told someone that I started to even understand that maybe it wasn't.'

'Jesus, Daisy, I had no idea.'

'Why would you? It's like with Ronnie, we all have stuff going on, all have things we have to deal with. The important thing is to not push it down or ignore it. You've got to deal with it or you'll never move on, believe me. Whatever it is you did, or think you did, I can handle it. Trust me.'

'I nearly killed him,' I blurted, before I could stop myself. 'My foster dad. I tried to kill him.'

As the words poured out of my mouth, I couldn't take my eyes off her reaction. I was looking for any emotion, any twitch of the mouth or loss of eye contact that told me I'd gone too far.

But there was nothing, just the same girl looking me in the eye, as hers glistened.

'What happened? It's OK. I'm still here, aren't I?'

'I'd been there about five or six months and it'd been difficult, but I was trying, you know? Every now and then I'd get lairy and key a car or something, but they knew about those things before I moved in. They knew what they were buying into. But I was starting to feel like it was home, that maybe they were happy with me. I had this amazing room . . . you should've seen it. It wasn't huge or anything, but it had a TV, stereo and the comfiest bed ever. I could sleep properly there and I've never done that, not that I can remember, anyway. I used to close my eyes and the next thing I knew, bang, it was morning. It was amazing.'

'Sounds it,' she replied, her eyes still holding mine.

'The couple were pretty sound as well. Bit stuck in their ways, but decent, you know? Every Wednesday night he'd go out to the pub, him and a couple of mates. Anyway, one night he went out as usual, so me and my foster mum sat in the lounge to watch a film. She'd made us popcorn and given me this huge glass of Coke as well. Don't know how much of the film I saw, though, because I fell asleep on the settee.'

I paused for a second or two, unsure of how I could go on without it sounding awful.

'It's all right, Bill, honest it is. You can tell me.'

'I don't really know what happened next. I remember some of it, but not very clearly, just kind of images and voices. He must have come home a couple of hours later and found us both asleep. Her in the chair and me on the settee. So he leaned over me and tried to carry me upstairs to bed, and that's when it happened.'

'What happened, Bill?'

I couldn't look her in the eye any longer.

'I went for him, didn't I? I mean, one minute I was asleep and the next minute there was someone leaning over me, stinking of whisky. I just freaked. Next thing I knew, we were both on the carpet, and I was whacking him again and again with this empty glass. I don't know how many times I did it, but it must have been a few, because the glass had broken and there was blood everywhere, all over me, all over him. With that, she woke up and pulled me away.'

I ran my hands through my hair and closed my eyes, terrified by what I'd just said, at how it must have sounded.

'I didn't mean to do it, though, Daisy. I didn't. I didn't know it was him. I thought it was . . .'

'Who?' she whispered. 'Who did you think it was?'

'I thought it was Shaun. Mum's boyfriend. He used to disappear for days at a time. Mum would freak out and hit the sauce, and leave me to fend for myself. Most nights I'd just fall asleep next to her on the settee, and that's where he'd find me when he finally showed up, full to the brim of whisky.'

'Jesus, Billy. What did he do to you?'

'You know. He'd just take his frustrations out on me. It didn't always last long, usually because he was too battered, but some nights, when he really had the devil in him, and if he was sober enough to get to his belt, well, it wasn't so good.'

Daisy shuffled closer to me and pushed her hands into mine.

'No wonder you reacted like you did. You can see that, can't you? It wasn't your fault, Billy.'

'It doesn't matter, though, does it? That was it, game over. I put him in hospital and within two hours the police were shoving all my stuff into bin liners. An hour after that and I was in Ronnie's car, on my way back home.'

'Did you see them again? The couple, I mean?'

'Oh aye, the scummers organized for us to meet a couple of weeks later. Not at their house, though. I wasn't allowed anywhere near that. We met at this centre, in this mad room. It was like something out of the loony bin, all soft furniture and rounded edges. Like they were worried I was going to go at them again. They did the whole routine about how it wasn't working, how it was as much to do with them as me. Bollocks. I wasn't the one with the caved-in face, was I?'

'And that was it, over?'

'Apart from Christmas and birthday cards, yeah. Not that he sends them. It's always her. Not that I blame him.'

'No, you just blame yourself.'

'What else can I do, Daisy? I was the one going mental, not him.'

'With good reason, Bill. Listen, you need to talk to someone about this. Someone who can help you with it.'

'What can they do? It happened. It's too late to change that now.'

'I know it is. But it's not too late to change how you feel about it. They can put it in perspective for you. Make you see that it's not your fault.'

I blew out of my mouth slowly, exhausted by finally letting it all out.

'You know what I want, Daisy? What I want more than anything?'

'What's that?'

'I just want to sleep. Sleep like I did while I lived there, that's all.'

She pulled my head on to her shoulder and wrapped her arms around me, squeezing so gently that she must have thought I was going to break.

CHAPTER 29

The last thing I needed was something else to think about, but as I stood outside Jan and Grant's, I was left with a difficult choice.

The car was still missing from the driveway and all the lights in the house were off. But where was the tactical light in the hallway?

I didn't know what to make of it, and with my head still banging from a combination of minesweeping and my earlier confession to Daisy, I was incapable of making a decision.

We'd spent the rest of the day together, trawling round town, checking out some DVDs she wanted to buy, just to kill a bit of time until the pubs got busy. I'd wandered after her, trying to concentrate on what she was saying, although my mind was elsewhere.

Letting Shaun out of my head felt dangerous, like he was watching us from the shadows. It certainly hadn't helped to talk to Daisy about him. If anything, I felt worse: bruised and raw, anything but calm.

The trip to the pubs helped, though, and like before Daisy was in top minesweeping form. It was a roasting afternoon, which meant the beer gardens were all bursting, making it easier for us to go unnoticed. We'd spent until early evening trawling from boozer to boozer, lifting whatever we could, and the lager had certainly taken the edge off my anxiety.

But now, two hours after we'd said goodbye, the sun had disappeared, the beer fog had lifted and the fear had begun to pinch away at me again. There was no way I wanted to go home and sit in an empty room, so I'd slowly made my way to my old house, to find no one there.

My hand shook with nerves as I searched for the door key. I desperately wanted to be inside, wanted the reassurance of my old room, the comfort of my old bed, even if it was only for a minute or two. I scanned up and down the street, checking that they hadn't parked their old Escort somewhere else, but there was no sign of it.

For some reason, I still dithered, uneasy at the lack of light warning off burglars.

I winced as I weighed up the options. It was risky and I knew it, but my need was so great that I scampered up the driveway and slid the key into the door before I could change my mind.

I crept along the hallway, craning my head around the kitchen and dining-room doors to find them both dark. I thought about taking my trainers off, but with the threat of being rumbled still in my head, I left them on and made for the stairs.

The house smelt amazing. Oldfield always had a whiff of school or hospital about it, something antiseptic, whereas here you could smell the food in the kitchen, the laundry hung over the radiators to dry.

After checking the bathroom and their bedroom, I headed

for my old room, and paused a moment before easing open the door and searching for the bedside lamp behind it.

I flicked the switch and for a moment I thought I must have wandered into the wrong place. It looked all wrong. The pale walls and bedspread from my last visit were gone. Instead I was looking at violet-painted walls, covered with obscure-looking posters and photos.

Sickness forced its way up past my gut as I scoured the room. The bed was covered with a purple duvet and a dozen cushions were piled against the headboard. My old TV and stereo were there, but so was a DVD player, and beside it an untidy pile of films. I rifled through them, as if the answers to the room would be found in the titles. But of course they offered nothing.

My mind was racing, throwing up reasons for the room to look like it did. Perhaps Jan and Grant had split up and she was sleeping in here, or maybe they were skint and had taken in a lodger. But as much as I desperately wanted it to be true, I knew that it wasn't. Someone *had* moved in, but it wasn't an adult, and my heart stopped as the truth dawned on me.

I'd been replaced.

As the truth hit, I lost all sense of secrecy and started tossing things around the room. There had to be something in here that told me who had moved in. Maybe it was someone from school or, worse still, one of the other ex-lifers from Oldfield? Whoever it was, I had to find out, find a way of making their life hell for moving in on my patch.

And then I spotted something on the windowsill.

It was a camera. The type you could use for filming as well as taking pictures.

The shaking in my hand got worse as I picked it up. With the other hand, I grabbed at the discs stacked behind it, my eyes scouring the words that were scrawled upon their spines: 'Dad – Xmas 2007', 'The Lakes – 2006'.

And then the case that stopped my heart dead: 'Louie and Lizzie – life-story book'.

I think I laughed when I read it. At the ridiculousness that that case could possibly be in here. It wasn't until I'd rammed the disc into the camera and hit Play that I stopped laughing. As there, on the viewfinder screen, was me, sat in the twins' room.

I let out a cry as I hurled the camera against the wall, but by the time the shattered pieces hit the bed, the tears were beginning to mix with anger.

I ran over to the wall by the bed, where a load of photos were stuck to the wall. And it was there that I knew for sure.

Because in every photo there was Daisy.

Smiling down at me.

By the time I'd reached the tenth photo, she was no longer smiling, she was laughing, and by the dozenth, she may as well have been flicking me the Vs. My hand grabbed them one by one, ripping them down and tossing them to the floor.

As I pulled the final photo down, I stared at Daisy and the man in it, as they stood arm in arm. Daisy looked different, so happy, but the man, who I guessed was her dad, wore the expression I saw so often on her face. He looked distracted and there was an unmistakable look of sadness scratched in his eyes.

I screwed the photo into a ball, unable to feel any sympathy for her or her family.

All those months she had sat there on the bench, listening to me, as I told her everything there was to know about my life, and all that time she'd been living here. Not with *friends*, like she'd said, but here. Sleeping in my bed, taking my parents further and further away from me. I thought back to what we'd talked about earlier that day. I'd told her about what I'd done to Grant, so I must have mentioned their names, she must have known who I was talking about.

So why didn't she say anything?

How could she have spent the rest of the day talking nonsense and drinking with me, when she knew that she'd moved in on the people who had promised me everything?

I smashed my foot into the bedside cabinet, reducing it to shards of wood, and tipped over the bed, scattering the cushions to each corner of the room.

It was only as I ground the larger pieces of camera into the carpet that I heard the door slam below. I suppose I should have been scared, but getting out was the last thing on my mind. After everything that had gone on, all the talking and the promises of being there for me, she was just like the rest of them. In fact, she was worse. She'd known what this place meant, but she'd taken it anyway.

So what point was there in running? Instead I walked to the top of the landing and stepped slowly down the stairs.

There they were, the happy family, slipping their shoes off at the front door.

Jan saw me first and mouthed my name like she had seen a ghost.

Grant's head snapped upwards as he heard her gasp, and for a second I thought that he was going to run full pelt up the stairs to tackle me. Were it not for Daisy, I think he would have done.

It took her a second to realize what was going on, so I continued down the stairs, throwing the balled-up photo of her dad at her feet.

'Billy?' she whispered. 'What are you doing here?'

I saw Grant stiffen beside her as she said my name, while Jan's hands flew to her mouth in surprise.

'You know each other?' Jan cried. 'Daisy? How do you know Billy?'

'School,' Daisy whispered, unable to force out another word, which gave me my opportunity to jump in.

'Well, this is lovely, isn't it? You must introduce me to your *friends*, Daisy.'

I paused, just long enough for the bitterness to reach my voice. 'Tell you what, don't bother. We already know each other.'

Daisy's eyes flicked to Jan and Grant, as if she were trying to understand what was going on.

As if she didn't know.

'So how long have they promised you can stay, then?' I spat. 'Oh, don't tell me. They're going to adopt you? Well, they've certainly done a nice job with your room. I could barely recognize it. Much posher than they had it for me anyway.'

'Billy?' Daisy wailed as she threw further looks at the two adults. Christ, she was some actress. 'I didn't know. How could I know they were . . .'

'Give it a rest. Do you think I'm stupid or something? You must have been laughing your tits off these last few months. So why did you do it, eh? What kind of nutcase are you?'

'That's ENOUGH, Billy,' roared Grant, as he stepped between the two of us. 'If anyone's acting like a nutter it's you. What do you think you're doing here? How did you even get in?'

I threw the key at him, which bounced off his shoulder. I saw his temper flare and braced myself for his attack, which would have come had Jan not grabbed his arm.

'Do you know what?' he yelled, his face volcanic red. 'We should've known it was you. Whenever Daisy's come in from seeing this "friend" of hers, stinking of booze, we should've known!'

'Aye, that's right. It's been me leading her astray. Me who's got her smoking and nicking pints off tables in pubs. Because I'm bad news, I am. Damaged goods. You had it right all along, didn't you?'

'Billy?' It was Jan's turn to have a go. 'We've never called you damaged goods, you know that. When things broke down, it was just as hard for us. You have to believe that.'

'Course it was. Must have been awful for you to stay here in your comfy home. I don't know how you coped, I really don't.'

'We didn't, Billy. Can't you see that? But we had no choice. You put Grant in hospital. He had dozens of stitches in his face. If the glass had been six inches lower, you could have killed him!'

'Well, if I'd known that I would have aimed harder, wouldn't I?'

Daisy stumbled forward and picked up the crumpled

photograph from the bottom of the stairs, her hands shaking as she tried to smooth out the edges.

'I would have understood,' I yelled at her. 'If you'd just told me, I would've understood.'

But she wouldn't even look me in the eye. All she could do was stare at the photo and rub it.

'Don't ignore me. I'm talking to you. Why didn't you tell me? I thought we were mates. You told me I could trust you. I told you everything!'

But I'd lost her. She had slipped away inside herself again, before turning and padding through to the kitchen, with Grant following after.

'Billy?' It was Jan again. 'Billy. Come downstairs and talk to us.' Her hand was outstretched and her face pleading, like she was the one in pain, not me.

'I don't think so,' I said, my voice as hard as stone. 'You made your choice. What else is there to say?'

'We can see you've had a shock, though. We all have. So let's talk about it, eh? Daisy's been through a lot lately. It's only just a year since her dad passed and she's been struggling with it all. Me and Grant, well, we were pleased she'd found a friend, because she's been so much happier lately.'

I tried to scoff at her, pushing all my contempt out through my nose in a giant huff, but it sounded pathetic.

'It's true. But we couldn't have known it was you, could we? Just as she couldn't have known that you'd lived here. Come on, Bill, come down and let's talk it out. Please?'

Without thinking, I took the first step down the stairs, and as I did I saw the first tear fall down her cheek.

As her arms closed around me, I let my head rest on her

shoulder, the tears stinging again as old wounds reopened. My head hurt with a fury that I didn't know existed. Everything was so fucked up. How had everything got so fucked up?

As my breathing softened I could see Grant pacing the kitchen floor, a phone clamped to his ear. Jan was still whispering to me, telling me everything was going to be fine, but I'd tuned her out by the time his voice reached me.

'That's right, 56 Walton Street. What? Yes, that's right . . . No, we've got him . . . We caught him at it . . . We'll explain when you get here.'

Jan fell on her back as I pushed her away. Her head clattered against the radiator and she looked stunned for a second, until she saw the phone in her husband's hand.

'Oh, Grant,' she wailed. 'What have you done?'

I didn't wait around to find out. I knew the rozzers would be here in minutes.

I turned and ran for the door, grabbing the car keys from the table as I went.

CHAPTER 30

Believe it or not, I felt lucky as I gunned the car down the dual carriageway. Lucky that Grant had backed the car into the driveway, leaving me no worries about reversing out and away.

Lucky as well that Jan was such a terrible driver. Grant had always taken the mick out of her, reckoned the car wanted to turn back home after a couple of miles when she was behind the wheel. As a result, he'd bought an automatic, which suited me no end. Without gears, it was just like driving a dodgem. All I had to do was point and press.

I had no idea where I was going, but knew I had to get there quickly. The filth would have been at their house within minutes, especially if Grant had noticed the car was gone. I knew there was no chance I was going to outrun them, not in this car and not with the best part of five beers still sloshing around inside me.

Keeping my eyes on the rear-view mirror as well as the road ahead, I looked for the next turn-off and was pleased to see that it led to the retail park by the river.

Braking hard, I felt the car lurch beneath me but managed to keep it on two wheels as the tyres wailed. Thank God it had been a dry weekend, otherwise who knows where the car would have spun to?

As I reached a mini-roundabout, I scoured the area for a decent spot to dump the motor.

All the car parks were practically empty, which was no surprise given the late hour, but I needed a pitch that was hidden. If the rozzers couldn't find the car, they'd have less chance of finding me.

I spotted it after only a couple of minutes, a sign that read 'Delivery Bay'. Perfect. There was no way anyone would be unloading now, and as the bay was tucked behind the warehouse, it was unlikely anyone would find the car until the next day. I killed my speed as I rounded the building, before cutting the lights as well.

I stopped about thirty metres from the loading-bay doors but left the engine running as it dawned on me just what I had done. I might not have written off the motor, but I'd certainly written off any decent future. With the police on the way and Grant only too happy to grass me up, I could kiss goodbye to any more time at Oldfield, or any therapeutic unit for that matter. On this sort of form, I'd be looking at secure. I chewed it over in my head. What was the difference between home and secure? Apart from the fact that they'd actually turn a key at the end of the day, there'd be no difference. Both of them were prisons.

Resting my head on the steering wheel, I tried to think what to do next, but it was hopeless. There wasn't a single option I could choose that didn't involve the police. Whether I went home, whether I ran, or even if I went back to Grant's to fess up, I knew they'd catch me.

My head buzzed with the events of the past hour, and the shame that Daisy had played me all along. What I couldn't work out was why. What she possibly had to gain from lying to me. I thought about the things I'd told her. The secrets I'd shared. The scummers had spent thousands over the years trying to get me to open up to someone about Shaun and home, and I'd sat there and blabbed it all to someone just as screwed up as me.

Whichever way I looked at it, it was the final straw. I'd been played by everyone. The social workers, Annie, even Ronnie. They'd all conspired to leave me like this, on my own and on the way to the nick.

What was the point, then? What was the point of handing myself in? I'd seen it time and time again with other lifers. As soon as they'd had one brush with the law, it was only a matter of time before it was another, then another, and by the time they knew it, they were on the best part of a three-stretch.

The thought of it terrified me. I knew there'd be no other option but to follow the same way, and I knew, despite all the headbutts and insults that I threw about, that there was no way I could stomach it.

I felt the accelerator growl beneath my foot and my eyes drifted upwards to the cargo doors that stood metres away. I tried to work out how quickly I'd have to be driving, what impact I'd have to make to avoid ending up in prison. Pretty damned hard, I reckoned, but in my broken head it was worth a go.

I reached my right arm across me and released the seat belt from the clasp, feeling the strap slide back to the door, leaving me exposed.

I pressed the pedal again, heard the engine roar its approval and reached for the handbrake.

At first I thought my leg was shaking and I tried to ignore it, dismissing it as a moment of weakness, but then I realized it was coming from my pocket.

It was my phone vibrating. My first instinct was to ignore it, that it was just Daisy or Jan begging me to forgive them, or, worse still, the police telling me to hand myself in.

But when it stopped, only to start again within seconds, I grabbed it and stared at the screen. It wasn't a number I knew and it certainly wasn't Daisy.

I shouted in irritation at it – 'What? What do you want?' – as a tiny voice fought to be heard above the car's engine.

'Billy? Billy?'

My foot fell off the pedal as I recognized the voice.

'Louie? Is that you, mate?'

'Billy. Come quick, will you?'

'What is it, Lou? What's wrong?'

'It's my dad,' he cried. 'It's Shaun. He's back.'

CHAPTER 31

The chances of running into the rozzers didn't bother me as I sprinted down the bypass.

I reckoned they'd be looking for me in a stolen car, not on foot. There had been the option of driving to Annie's of course, but the risk was too great. If they caught me they were hardly going to agree to a detour, were they? My best chance was to leg it there, using as many shortcuts away from the main roads as possible.

I had it all mapped out in my head and reckoned I could be there in fifteen minutes, although by the time I reached the allotments, I was starting to run out of steam – hardly surprising given the drinking that had gone on. Pushing my legs onwards, I refused to stop, Louie's terrified voice ringing in my ears: *Hurry, Billy, hurry.*

All kinds of craziness were going on in my head. What was Shaun doing there? Had Annie been planning it all along? And what had he already done to make Lou so scared? With every step I focused on his name, and the snarling face that had haunted me throughout my boxing sessions with the Colonel.

I'd carried what he'd done to me every day for the last

ten years. It had eaten away at me, fuelled my anger, left me unable to trust anyone or anything, but now he was back, I wasn't going to let him repeat history with the twins.

The tower blocks that lined the edge of the ghost estate veered into view and for once the area lived up to its name. The streets were empty, silent except for the slapping of my trainers against the pavement. The sound echoed off the tower-block walls, pushing back a beat that drove me on quicker still, and it wasn't until I reached the corner of Forbes Ave that I allowed myself to stop.

My hands fell to my knees as I bent double, gasping for air. I knew I had to take a second or two to steady myself, think about what I was going to do when I reached the door.

As I walked up the path my heart was going mental. I couldn't believe I was here, or help remembering my promise to Annie that I would never set foot in the house again. At least I had been right about one thing. Only bad stuff went on in there. Crouching, I edged my way along, past the front door to the lounge window. Wrapping my fingers round the ledge, I eased myself upright, daring to peek through the window. Instantly I saw him, or rather the back of him, as he stood just metres from me, waving his arms wildly, bottle of whisky in hand.

I tried to scan the room, see where the twins were, check that they were all right, but I couldn't see them, so, lowering myself, I scuttled down the path at the side of the house, towards the back door.

As I approached the door, my heart leapt as I saw it ajar. Knowing he wouldn't be able to see me from the kitchen, I teased the door open, to be confronted by his voice, the same rasping noise as all those years ago. It was thick with booze and smoke, a croak rather than a voice. But in a way that seemed right – he was an animal, not a human being.

Peeking through the gap, I could see him towering over Annie and Lizzie, who were huddled together on the carpet, pushed into the corner by the TV. I don't know who looked more scared, mother or daughter. Annie had a bruise over her left eye, and her arms wrapped tightly around Lizzie, who flinched with every word that came out of Shaun's mouth.

'What I don't understand, Annie,' he slurred, waving his arms excitedly, 'is how you thought you could keep it from me. I mean, this is big news. Our babies back home again, where they belong.'

Believe me, there was no joy in his voice. Every word was loaded with hate, each word a bullet aimed straight at Annie.

'But that's you all over, isn't it, eh? You always were a spiteful cow. Never wanted me to be involved, did you?'

With that he kicked her. A full-blooded boot that crumpled Annie into a ball and sent Lizzie scrabbling behind her.

'Tell you what,' he added. 'How's this for a plan? I don't have to stay here, you know? I've got my own place now on the other side of town. It isn't fancy or nothing, but it's got two bedrooms. Enough space for me and my boy. What d'you reckon, son?' He swung his arm around Louie, who must have been stood in front of him, out of my sight. 'A boy needs his dad, not these bloody airy-fairy social workers. They don't know shit!'

I saw Louie flinch as Shaun's arm clung to his shoulder,

but alongside the fear in his face I could see something else that looked liked repulsion, like anger.

'I'm not going anywhere with you,' he spat, before pulling his arm away. 'You aren't my dad and never will be neither.'

Louie didn't see the blow coming. It arced round from wide and caught him below the eye, sending him crashing into a coffee table, which spilt its lamp to the floor.

Before I knew it I was through the door and at him, but not before Annie cried out my name in shock.

Shaun spun around before I could land a blow on him, his face twisting from anger to surprise as his brain worked out who he was looking at.

'Bloody hell,' he said, and laughed, his grin twisted and demonic. 'Billy? Is that you? Well, look at this, will you? The whole family's back together.'

When my hands made contact with his chest, I could feel how drunk he was, as he lost his balance and wobbled backwards on to the settee.

'Steady on, Bill!' he complained. 'That's no way to treat your old man, is it?'

'Louie had it right,' I spat, my finger pointed at his chest. 'You're no father, not to him and certainly not to me.'

'I took you and your mother in, though, didn't I? Gave you a roof over your head, which is more than any other bugger ever did.'

'Didn't give you the right to crack me, though, did it, Shaun? Didn't give you the right to beat me whenever you fancied it?'

'It wasn't every night,' he wailed as he pulled himself to

his feet. 'There were times that you needed pulling into line, that's all.'

'Pulling into line? You beat me so hard Annie couldn't take me outside the house for weeks at a time. She had to hide me away like she was ashamed of me.'

I chanced a glance over at Annie as the tears poured down her face.

'That's because she *was* ashamed of you. You were always a sour little shit. Never smiling, always with a long face on you.'

'Is there any wonder,' I yelled, 'with you constantly off your face?'

He burped as he took a long swig of his whisky, his breath as evil as he was.

'I was only doing what my dad taught me. All right, I haven't exactly set the world on fire, but at least I know what discipline is.'

I'd heard enough of his crap. The booze had screwed his body and his mind, so I turned and went to pick up Louie, who was cowering by the settee.

As soon as I lifted him to his feet, I felt Shaun's hands on my shoulders.

'Oi!' he shouted. 'Did I say you could touch him? Take your hands off. If you want anything to do with him, you ask me, you hear?'

He grabbed at Louie and swung him towards Annie, before turning his attention to me.

He must have seen the anger flare in my eyes, as a sneer licked up his face.

'Oh, I see. Now you've grown up, you think you can take

your old man, do you? Fancy your chances, do you? Well, come on, then, Billy. What are you waiting for?'

I don't know if he saw the punch coming or not, but his reactions certainly weren't quick enough to stop it. My right hand smashed against his cheek, but I felt no pain as he sprawled across the settee, a small cut opening beneath his left eye.

Without hesitating, I was on top of him.

This was it.

This was the moment I'd visualized all those times with Ronnie.

The moment I could get him back.

Hurt him the way he'd hurt me.

But as I sized up another punch, he let one of his own go, which caught me on the chin and knocked me backwards.

The years of drink may have diluted his physical size, but it had done nothing but breed anger in him, and he roared as he reared above me, sending another punch flush into my nose.

The punch lacked power, but my eyes watered as I raised my hands to my face, trying to stop any more shots from reaching me. I had to get him off me, so I pulled my legs up to my chest and catapulted them against his body, sending him sprawling to the floor. Ignoring the blood dripping from my nose, I jumped on top of him and pinned his arms under my knees, leaving him at my mercy.

'Do you have any idea how long I've waited for this?' I yelled.

My eyes were on fire and as they flicked around the room they saw the lamp that Louie had knocked to the ground.

Carefully, I leaned to my left and grabbed the flex of the lamp, before pulling the base into my hand like a club.

'Do you know how often I've dreamed of being able to do this to you?'

'Do you honestly think I give a shit, Billy? You really think I care what you think of me? I never have cared and I never will. So do what you want, mate. Another beating isn't going to make one shred of difference.'

His eyes rolled in his head and I felt the alcohol force his body into submission. He was broken, a shrivelled version of the violent, drunken man he'd been, and as I lifted the lamp above my head he simply closed his eyes in defeat.

The adrenalin pumped in my ears as I gripped the lamp harder and harder. I looked for the perfect spot to make contact with, knowing I was only centimetres away from what I'd been dreaming about.

I don't know why I hesitated then. Maybe I could feel the twins looking, or maybe it was just sheer exhaustion catching up with me. But I did pause, and I let my head turn to where they were bundled. And as soon as I saw them, saw their eyes, I knew I wasn't going to hit him again.

There was such fear on their faces, and it was a fear that I knew. It was the fear I had felt every time Shaun had come anywhere near me. And now it was their fear too, as they watched me, lamp in hand, about to bring it down on his head.

Breathing deeply, I let my arm fall and the lamp slid to the ground.

That was it.

All the violence, all the fighting.

Finished.

I didn't want it any more, didn't want them to have to see it either, to grow up thinking it was the normal thing to do.

Instead, I wiped the blood away from my mouth and risked a smile, although God knows what it must have looked like.

'Louie? You still got that phone?'

Louie nodded, his eyes still fearful.

'Good. I need you to ring Ronnie. You know the number. Tell him I'm here and that he needs to come and collect us.'

'Where are we going, Bill?' Lizzie asked, her face flushed with tears.

'Home for now,' I replied, the words catching in my throat. 'We're going home.'

CHAPTER 32

The fallout was immediate and seemed to last for weeks. After enough time had passed, Ronnie always joked that they'd felt the tremors in France.

At first, though, it was just plain terrifying.

As we waited for the Colonel to arrive, I stood over Shaun, worrying that he'd break out of his stupor and have another go at the four of us. But although he'd moaned and rubbed at the bruises on his face, he made no attempt to do a runner.

When Ronnie arrived, he wasn't on his own. He burst in with half a dozen rozzers, like some kind of middle-aged SAS platoon. The officers were properly confused by the sight of me, a bloody-nosed version of the kid they were already looking for, and at first I thought they were going to slap cuffs on me. But then the Colonel took control and, to be fair to him, he was pretty awesome. In fact, you'd have thought *he* was the commanding officer the way he redirected the rozzers towards Shaun instead of me.

It took them a few minutes to get him restrained and on his feet, and I could see the twins flinching further behind Annie as he lurched through the door, yelling some nonsense that he alone understood. It was only when the doors to the riot van closed and it tore away up the street that they dared to appear again, their faces stained with tears.

The next few minutes were a whirl of sirens and people, as the room flooded with police, paramedics and social workers. Dawn arrived, looking like she'd stumbled into her own worst nightmare, and when she caught sight of Annie, still crumpled on the floor, I thought she'd need treatment herself.

The paramedics were trying to help Annie, but were struggling to get past the twins, who were clinging to her. When they tried to prise them off, their cries increased and left Annie trying to bat the medics away.

I leaned down, putting my arms around them both.

'You need to let them have a look at Annie,' I said softly. 'She'll be OK, but you need to give her a minute or two, right?'

Reluctantly they followed me, though Lizzie refused to let her eyes leave her mum for a second.

As I sat them on the settee, I checked them out for any obvious damage, relief washing over me as I realized that, apart from a small bruise on Louie's cheek, they were both OK.

The same couldn't be said for Annie. She yelped as they touched her ribs and her breathing was short and troubled. It was obvious she was going to hospital, but the twins reacted badly when Dawn told them. Lizzie dashed back to her, clung desperately to her hand and refused to let go.

'It's all right, Lizzie,' Dawn whispered. 'I think it would

be best if both you and Louie went to the hospital with Mum. We need to get you all checked over.'

Once they'd wheeled Annie out to the ambulance, with the twins huddled on either side, attentions turned to me.

'That's some night you've had,' said one of the rozzers, as a paramedic shone a light into my eyes. 'We're going to need you to come with us and explain what's gone on. And I don't mean just here either.'

'Hang on a minute,' interrupted Ronnie. 'The lad's gone through a lot and you can see how worried he is about the twins. Do us a favour, will you? Let him have the once-over at the hospital, make the sure the twins are OK. Then I'll have him straight down to talk to you.'

'We'll need to see him the minute he's finished. He's a lot to fill us in on.'

'I realize that. You have my word. He'll be with you the second he's done.'

The journey to hospital was a quiet one.

Although I knew there was nothing wrong with me, I was more than happy to go along for the ride. It bought me some time to think about what I'd say to the police, but more importantly it meant I could keep an eye on the twins.

They were in a right state by the time we arrived. Annie's injuries were worse than first thought. Something about internal bleeding, so they'd whipped her off sharpish for more tests, which left the twins alone with Dawn, who was struggling to keep them happy.

After half an hour or so, we'd calmed them down enough to let a doctor take a look at them, and apart from their frazzled nerves there was nothing physical to report. Louie's face was bruised, but there was no sign of concussion. The only scars he had would be in his head.

I knew all about them and knew I'd let him down. That if I'd got there quicker, they could have been avoided.

Once they'd been given the all clear, we were left with the next problem: how to get them home calmly without me? After all, there was no way the Colonel was going to break his word to the rozzers, and as for Annie, well, she wasn't going anywhere, not that night.

It killed me, it did. Seeing their reaction when they heard I had to go and see the police.

Louie grabbed on to my waist, and when Ronnie tried to break his grip, he wailed and cried. He was so desperate to hang on to me that he even tried to bite the Colonel's hands as he pulled him away. Lizzie was no calmer either. She fought Dawn with every ounce of strength she had until a couple of nurses carried her through reception and out to a waiting car. Her screams of 'Billy' bounced off every wall, making my ears ring with pain.

They needed me. Now more than ever. And the only place I was heading was the police station. As Ron led me out to his car, I couldn't help wondering if I'd see anything that night except for a cell.

It felt like dawn by the time the rozzers got round to talking to me. It wasn't of course, but they left me to stew for a couple of hours before ripping a strip off me.

Ronnie sat beside me as we waited, prodding me into the details of what had gone on before arriving at Annie's. What I'd done to land myself in so deep.

He didn't look shocked when I told him. Or angry either. He just looked old and tired, and for the second time in two days he looked human.

'I don't know what to say, Bill.' He sighed, rubbing at his eyes. 'I just don't understand what you thought you were doing, breaking in there. I can't protect you when you do things like that. You know that, don't you?'

I nodded slowly, keeping my eyes on the floor. It felt like a week had passed since the confrontation at their place. I'd been so focused on getting to the twins quickly that it was only just dawning on me why I was here, and what I'd let myself in for.

An hour later I was under no illusion. The rozzers had given it to me both barrels, reeling off a list of stuff I could be done for: breaking and entering, burglary, criminal damage, assault, car theft . . . By the time they'd finished, I reckoned they'd be ready to throw away the key.

And that's when Ron jumped in, but instead of giving me a kicking, he started defending me.

Giving them the hard sell about everything I'd gone through. Not just about the twins leaving, but how I'd been abandoned by Annie, about the adoption breaking down, about the strides I'd taken to sort myself out.

Gobsmacked, I was. Speechless. It was like he was talking about someone else, how he'd speak up for one of his boys. His precious, precious boys.

By the time he finished, even the police seemed to be wavering, but not enough to let me walk out with a smacked wrist as a warning.

'We appreciate that Billy's made progress recently, but

let's be frank, it's not the first time we've had to speak to him about criminal damage. We have to look at the mess he's created in the space of one evening. The upset he's caused to a family. A family who offered him a chance in the past. You have to understand their point of view.' All eyes fixed on me. 'You can understand how they feel, can't you, Billy?'

I nodded, regardless of the emotions that flicked through my mind.

'All I can say is that you can go home with Ronnie now, but we'll be calling you back in as soon as we have a full statement from the Scotts. You've overstepped the mark, Billy, and this isn't the sort of behaviour that can be shrugged off with yet another warning.'

The journey home was even quieter than the one to the station.

I knew there was no way Jan and Grant were going to let me off the hook this time and now we were on our own the Colonel seemed less forgiving than he had in front of the police.

His angry silence said everything and it was a silence I didn't dare break. So when my phone buzzed in my pocket I turned it off and continued to stew over the mess I'd created.

The twins were home and safe. But it didn't look like I would be there long enough to enjoy it.

CHAPTER 33

I felt like I'd been in a war when I woke the next morning. I don't know what had crippled me more, the punches I'd taken from Shaun or the night's sleep on the floor outside the twins' room.

Not that there'd been a lot of sleeping going on. The scummers had struggled to get the twins settled when they got back and when I went in to check on them I managed to wake them again. Can't say that went down well with the Colonel. After giving me a stare that would shatter glass, he disappeared down to the study. God knows how much paperwork I'd created for him. A couple of pens' worth at least.

Eventually the twins had settled, but I just drifted in and out of fitful sleep, and dreams of sharing a cell with Shaun.

Ronnie woke me by nine o'clock, plonking a steaming tea beside me.

'I thought I'd better wake you up before one of the other kids did it themselves.' His face was impassive, no sign of the ice thawing in his voice. 'Get that down you, then jump in the shower. It might sort you out a bit.'

He was right. I turned the water as hot as I could stand

and let the spray batter me, easing out the tension that I'd been holding in my shoulders. Only when the tank was empty and the water ran cold did I get out, ready to face the mess that I thought would be waiting for me.

As it turned out, no one said much to us that day. Ronnie spent most of it holed up in the office, and whenever I tried to grab a word with him, he shooed me away, the phone clamped between his shoulder and ear.

It was mid-afternoon by the time he appeared and even then his focus was on the twins.

'Right, grab your coats, you two. I thought you might want to go and see your mum at the hospital.'

The twins bounded to the cloakroom, smiles pasted to their faces for the first time that day.

'And you need to stay inside, Billy, you hear? Part of your bail depends on you being housebound, so I'd suggest you do as you're told for once.'

I didn't fancy going out anyway. I mean, where was I going to go? It wasn't as if I had anyone I wanted to go and see. Not any more.

I spent the next hour balled up on my bed, trying to sleep, but when that didn't happen, I switched on my phone instead, to be faced with the message I'd ignored the night before.

It was from Daisy:

```
Call me. I didn't know. You must know
that? I'm sorry, D
```

I hit delete instinctively, though I couldn't work out if I wiped it out of anger or embarrassment. What was she playing at? How could she claim to have been in the dark about Jan and Grant? How could she not have realized?

I tried to replay our conversations back in my head. Tried to remember the number of times I'd talked about them. How many times had I mentioned them by name? I must have done. I just couldn't remember when.

I reckoned that by deleting the message I could put it out of my head. Forget about the doubts that were invading my thoughts. But Daisy wouldn't let it go. The texts kept coming. Not every hour or anything, but a couple of times a day for the next three days:

```
U have to believe me. I didn't know. Y
would I lie to u?
```

But they didn't stay so calm for long. Four or five messages in, they were more typically Daisy:

```
What is yr problem? Doesn't the truth
matter 2 u? Sort it out and call me
```

So what did I do?

I bottled it and threw every spare thought I had into the twins.

It was like we were living in limbo. I suppose we were all in shock as well.

The twins in particular didn't know their arses from their elbows and were twitchy whenever someone new came into view. You could hardly blame them.

The Colonel came and went with his shifts, but spent a

lot of time on the phone behind closed doors, or down the hospital with the twins. It wasn't until five days on that he sat us down with Dawn, and my heart raced with anticipation as he told us what he'd been working on.

'I'm so sorry, you know,' he said, sighing sadly, 'that you've had to go through the last few days. You didn't deserve it and, in so many ways, it's *our* fault. If we had any idea that Shaun was still around, then we'd have played it so differently.'

The twins huddled closer to me, freaked by the mention of his name.

'One thing we are sure of,' he continued, 'is that your mum didn't play a part in him turning up like that. From the way she's reacted to all this, that's obvious. She's taken it very hard, you know? She'd worked a long time to get herself straight, but she's going to need a little bit of time again now, just to get herself back on track, and so we can monitor her.'

'We can still see her, though, can't we?' asked Lizzie.

'Of course you can,' soothed Dawn, taking over the reins. 'Our plan is still,' and at that moment she focused on me, her eyes a mixture of fear and regret, 'to have the two of you back home with her. But, as Ronnie says, we can't put a time on that. It could be a month or two, but it could be longer. Whenever it is, it will be when it's right for your mum, but more importantly, when it's right for you.'

My heart sank, although it was only what I was expecting. I'd seen Annie's face that night, the fear in her eyes, and although I knew she was still capable of putting on a front, she wasn't that good an actress.

Dawn rambled on for a bit about support and counselling, but didn't mention anything to do with Jan and Grant in front of the twins, which was a relief.

Neither Ronnie nor me had breathed a word of it to them, not with everything else they were dealing with. It wasn't until she sent the twins off to watch some telly that the conversation turned to me.

'Right, Bill,' Ron said, shifting his weight forward in his chair. 'We need to talk about your mess as well.'

I held his gaze, knowing whatever was coming my way would be pretty much deserved.

'What you did, Bill, at Jan and Grant's, was unacceptable. You know that, don't you?'

I nodded slowly.

'Unacceptable to me, to them, but most importantly to the police. Regardless of whether you had a key or not, and believe me, I don't want to know how you got it or even how many times you used it, you were breaking and entering. It's not your house any more, Billy, do you understand me?'

I nodded again.

'Which brings me on to their car. What in God's name did you think you were doing? You're fifteen years old. Do you realize what would've happened if you'd had a crash, hurt someone, killed someone even? You do realize just how much trouble you're in, don't you?'

'Course I do. And I'm sorry. I just lost the plot when I found Daisy . . .'

'I don't want to hear it, Bill. Whatever your reason is, it can't justify the way you behaved. Whatever it is that's

255

happened with Daisy, you need to deal with it, because, what I hear, she needs a friend right now.'

'What do you mean?' I asked, my interest pricked. 'Have you spoken to her?'

'No, of course I haven't. But I have spoken to Jan and Grant. In fact, I've spoken to them more than my own wife these last few days.'

'And what did they say? About Daisy?'

The sight of her face as she smoothed out the photo of her dad was still fresh in my mind.

'If you want to know about Daisy, then you'll have to speak to her. What you need to be worrying about is the Scotts. Grant in particular.'

'Is he still pissed off?'

'That doesn't even cover it, Billy. I mean, how did you feel when you saw Shaun in Annie's house, when he had no right to be there?'

I couldn't look him in the eye as I understood what he meant.

'You broke into his house, smashed up a room, assaulted his wife and stole his car. You're lucky he's not been round here himself.'

'Maybe I should talk to him, then?' I said, although the prospect filled me with fear.

'I don't think that's a good idea, Billy. Not after all the good work me and Dawn have been doing.'

'What do you mean?'

'As I said, we've been talking to him a lot, to the both of them. And we've managed to get him to drop the charges.'

'You've what?'

'It wasn't easy. In fact, you've got Jan to thank more than us. She's the one who talked Grant round.'

I felt my entire body relax, although my head was spinning.

'I don't understand,' I stammered. 'How did you manage it?'

'We told them the truth, about the twins going back to Annie and how devastated you were, about how you'd changed over the last few months, about how you wouldn't last five minutes in secure, no matter what you think!'

I felt a wave of shame rush over me, as the extent of what Ron had done hit home. He was right. I couldn't cope with going away, I'd known that all along.

Ronnie pulled me back from my thoughts.

'Don't you think for a second that you've got away with it. Because the first thing you're going to do is write them the longest, most sincere letter you can, explaining why you did it and, most importantly, how you're going to put it right.'

I looked quizzically at him.

'You're going to pay them back, Bill. For the broken camera, for any damage to Daisy's room and their car. And you're going to pay for a new set of locks to their house as well. Do you understand?'

I felt like a recruit on the training ground as he ripped into me, and I nodded, wondering how long it would take me to get that sort of money together, but knowing anything was better than secure.

'Is that it?' I asked, knowing I had a long letter to think about.

'No. There are three more things,' he barked. 'First, you've still got to come to the police station with me. The charges may have been dropped, but they want to have words anyway about your joyriding. This is a last chance, Billy. You understand that, don't you?'

I nodded silently.

'The second thing,' he added, his face still grim as he stepped forward, 'is about something Annie told me.'

I frowned, hoping this wasn't the start of more mind games as she tried to get the twins home again.

'I know all about the lamp, Billy. I know you were going to hit Shaun with it, but I also know you decided against it. I just wanted to tell you I'm proud of you for making that choice.'

I felt the heat rise in my cheeks.

'Do you know what makes me most proud?'

I didn't have a clue.

'It's that six months ago I think you'd have gone through with it. I don't think you'd have thought twice about cracking him with it. And that shows me how much you've changed. I know you might not see that yet, and I wouldn't blame you, it's been a mental few months. But believe me, you will.'

I turned to leave, hoping he was right.

'Oi. I haven't finished with you yet.'

I faced him again, wondering what else there was to say. But he didn't say anything.

Instead, he held out his hand and passed me an envelope.

I looked at it, confused. There was no writing on it. Nothing.

'What's this?' I asked.

The Colonel just smiled and gave me a gentle, playful shove towards the door.

It was silent in the garage. No other lifers tearing round. Or scummers clock-watching as the final minutes of their shift crawled by. It was just me and the little world that Ron had built. I'd spent a bit of time in there since it all kicked off, working at the bag, punching out the frustrations that were nibbling at me.

The only difference was Shaun.

He hadn't vanished.

He was still there when I hit the bag, but he didn't seem to sneer as hard as he had, and I didn't need to punch myself into submission before he faded away.

But tonight wasn't about punching. Or training. It was all about the letter. About whether I wanted to open the envelope.

I knew what it said. It had to be from Grant, warning me. Keep away from my family and all that, and to be honest I didn't need to hear it. But I knew chucking it wasn't an option either. Not when Ronnie was bound to ask me about it.

So I slid my finger into the fold and ripped it open, my eyes falling on to writing that wasn't Grant's.

No, I'd seen this handwriting before. In class.

Dear Billy,

I can't believe I've resorted to writing to you. I think the last letter I wrote was to Father Christmas, and he never brought me what I asked for. So why I think this is going to work with you – well, to be honest, I don't. But I had to try, you know?

I just need you to understand one thing, Billy.

There's one thing that I need you to believe.

I didn't know about Jan and Grant. That you even knew them, never mind had been fostered by them. I mean, I don't know how you expected me to know.

Whenever you talked about 'that' family, you never mentioned names. It was hard enough for you to even acknowledge they existed, never mind go into details.

I promise you, Billy, if you had said their names, or if I'd cottoned on to who they were, don't you think I would have mentioned it? Do you really think I could've kept the shock off my face?

And besides, having you around has been good.

I mean, you're a pain in the arse, always bugging me, asking me questions about what's gone on in the past.

But you know what?

If it means you'll believe me, I'll tell you.

All of it.

My mum and dad are dead.

Mum died giving birth to me, and all my life, as long as I can remember, I've felt it was my fault. Don't bother telling me I'm being daft. My dad told me the same, but I could never shake it off, you know? How could I?

So it was always just me and Dad.

And then he died, in a car crash. And the only reason he was in the car was me.

So it felt like I killed him too. Just like I did Mum.

And now I'm on my own. All right, I have Jan and

Grant, but that's not enough. Never will be, no matter
what they do.

So you know, it would be good if you read this to the
end, and then you might get it into your head that I might
be worth trusting. That I might be telling the truth.
Because the way I see it, Billy Finn, we could do with
being mates, me and you.

But I'm not going to beg.
And I'm not going to text you any more.
It's up to you.
Get in touch if you can,
Dx

I don't think I breathed all the time I was reading.

Or for the minute after.

Instead, I sat and tried to make sense of her words, applying them to conversations we'd had. To the times when she'd
looked so vacant.

Minutes passed. It might even have been an hour. But
suddenly it came to me.

What I needed to do.

It wouldn't take long. But I needed to be in my room to
do it.

So I slipped out of the garage, locked the door and headed
back across the lawn.

There was so much to think about as I lay in bed that night.
Everything had changed, but in some ways everything had
stayed the same.

The twins were back, but were probably going. The

Colonel was here and I knew that he cared, but in hours he'd be going home to his family.

And as for me, well, nothing had changed.

I was still Billy Finn, lifer.

I was still a resident at Oldfield House and would be until they kicked me out at eighteen.

But I knew that I'd been given a chance. I had no idea what I was going to do with it, but I knew it was there all the same. I had to prove something, to the twins, to Annie and to Ronnie, and although it scared me, at least it was in my hands.

I'd started my letter to Jan and Grant earlier, and as per usual Ronnie had stuck his nose in, complaining it didn't 'kiss nearly enough arse'. So it was back to square one.

Although I knew that was the letter I had to write first, the message I really wanted to send was to Daisy, and as I lay on my back in the darkness, I didn't have a clue where to start.

What I did know was that I would have to work it out.

I didn't need reminding that I needed to find the words to say sorry.

After all, there was now a single star, shining from my ceiling, that wouldn't ever let me forget.

ACKNOWLEDGEMENTS

Thanks for reading about Billy. The anxiety and isolation that he endures during the book are feelings that many people, young and old, experience. What's important is not to suffer alone. There are people out there who can help, and great websites like *www.thecalmzone.net* that offer superb non-judgmental advice and support.

So many people have encouraged and cajoled over the years, and I owe you all a great deal. Big old thanks to Boz, Cally, Philippa, Lel, Charlie Sheppard, Ali Jensen, James Heneage and 'Slasher' Gash.

Cheers to my friends who put up with my grumpiness and agoraphobia with a humour that belies belief. In particular, Esther, Haydn, Oscar, Robyn, Waggy, Finigan, Katy, Matt, Charlie, Kisia, Scott, Big Bad Brown, Charlotte, Emma (paperweight champion of Peckham), David Philips and JJ, Pee Dee, Vic, Zoe, Lou, Matthew, Nicola, Henry and Anna, Will, Burto, Benton and Burb.

Huge thank you to my brilliant parents, Ray and Neet, to Jonathan, Hen, Yasmin and the other members of the clan up in the frozen North. Much love also to my outlaws, Sheil and Pete, Paul and Jacky for their unwavering support, and to Bob, Jo, Edie, Pooch and Shreeve-o for not ripping it out of me too mercilessly.

Everyone at work has been incredibly supportive and patient. HUGE thanks to Rob Cox, whose endless encouragement spurred me on to not only get started but keep going ('That's right . . .!'), but also to the fabulous Dawn Burnett, Ally, Shipp, Shell, Charlotte, Jones Christine Jones, Dominic, Grainne, Gill, SJV, Sarah, Sophie, Emma (and Ed) for the red pen, Nick Stearn, and the ever-wise Mr and Mrs C.

To Becky Stradwick, who didn't groan when I asked her to read early chapters – I thank you. We've cooked up some schemes over the years, but this is the best one yet. Thank you for getting me this far before jumping overboard!

I'm so grateful to everyone at the Darley Anderson Agency, especially my agent Madeleine Buston for the title, and for sneaking Billy into places he never thought he'd reach.

Thanks also to Richard Mac, Helen MS, The Hough, Kevin, Jen, Emily, Annie, Barry, Rachel Airey, Kate Hancock, Claudia Mody, John Newman, Helen Masterton, Trish and Jacky, Graham Marks, Sophie Mckenzie and Jenny Downham. All of you have been so supportive. I hope you know that I appreciate it.

To the publishing team at Puffin – thank you. In particular, Sarah, Jennie, Lesley, Kirsty, Jacqui, Katy, and especially to my editor, Shannon Park, who from noodles onwards, has been nothing shy of magnificent.

Much love and thanks also to Dawn, Claire, Dominic, Mally, Dave, Janice, Frank and all my old friends from the Sailors' Families' Society, and to Eric de Mel, whose friendship meant so much.

My love as well to Jonny and Astri John-Kamen, who know why, and I hope will never forget.

But most of all, thanks to my missus, Laura, for reminding me there's still the washing-up to be done.

And to Albie Johnson and Elsie Jeane, I love you. No matter what time of night it is . . .

Gipsy Hill, June 2010